• • • • • • • • •

The Secret Under the Whirlpool

Elaine Breault Hammond

RAGWEED
THE ISLAND PUBLISHER

For my grandchildren: Emily, Erica, Desmond, Kristen and Craig.

Second Printing, 1998

Edited by: Jennifer Glossop
Cover and book illustrations: Mary Montgomery
Printed and bound in Canada by: AGMV Marquis

Ragweed Press acknowledges the generous support of the Canada Council of the Arts.

Published by:
Ragweed Press
P.O. Box 2023
Charlottetown, P.E.I.
Canada   C1A 7N7

Canadian Cataloguing in Publication Data

Hammond, Elaine Breault, 1937–

   The secret under the whirlpool

   ISBN 0-921556-61-6

I. Title.

P8565.A566S43 1996   jC813'.54   C96-950137-4

PZ7.H36Se 1996

Contents

Chapter One

The Voice in the Wind

The sun was bright, and the water of the bay was flat and shining like a mirror — but only for a moment. A puff of warm breeze scuffed across its surface, breaking it into tiny ripples and causing a restless slap of water at the shoreline. *Slap*, pause, *slap*.

A thin girl, her long brown hair pulled back from her face because of the heat, was sprawled on her stomach on a grassy bank above the beach. Her chin on her hand, she was staring across the bay as if hypnotized. The only sound she could hear at first was the water against the stones. Then she heard a faraway roar, building and fading, building and fading. She knew at once the sound had been there from the first, and it frightened her a little. She cocked her head to one side, listening hard.

Aunt Kate shifted in her lawn chair, and a book slid from her lap to the grass, waking her. She took off her straw hat and balanced it on her bony knee. Running her fingers through her short gray hair, she stretched and turned toward the girl.

"What's that sound?" Maggie asked her.

"What?" Aunt Kate said in a sleepy voice.

"Shh. Listen. The roaring."

"It's the surf. The ocean rolling onto the beach. Way out there, where the bay opens to the sea — to the Gulf of St. Lawrence, actually. We'll go swimming there sometime."

Maggie yawned. Going swimming with Aunt Kate was not an exciting prospect. All spring she had been looking forward to her holidays on Prince Edward Island, but that had been when Uncle Jeff had been coming, too.

She remembered the day, early in the spring, when Uncle Jeff had burst into the house, as happy and full of energy as a Newfoundland pup, waving a fistful of tourist brochures in front of her. Wind surfing, clam digging, horseback riding. They would do all these things on Prince Edward Island. They would stay for the whole month of July. Every night they would have a bonfire on the beach in front of the cottage he had rented. And her best friend, Colleen, could come, too. They could keep each other company when he was occupied with his business meetings.

"Wow, that's fantastic!" she had laughed back. A whole month in a cottage by the seaside with Uncle Jeff and Colleen, the only two people in the world who really cared about her since her mother died.

She also clearly remembered the day, a few weeks later, when Uncle Jeff came home looking serious.

"I'm sorry, Maggie, but I just got an invitation to give a lecture at a conference in Vancouver. I'm going to spend most of July out there, setting up meetings."

"Does this mean you can't come to the Island?" she had asked in a small, controlled voice.

"I'm afraid so," he said, reaching out to take her hand. "Try to understand. It's a perfect opportunity to expand my business to the other side of the country."

Maggie scowled. "You're always going away on business trips," she said, pulling her hand away. "I hardly ever see you."

"That's an exaggeration," said Uncle Jeff. "Besides, don't I always bring you something special when I come home?"

"Don't go," she had begged.

"I'm sorry, but I must," he said firmly. "But this doesn't mean you have to give up your holiday. You and Colleen can still go to the Island. You'll have a wonderful time. And, of course, Aunt Kate will be there to keep an eye on you."

A few days later Colleen had called to say her parents wanted her to go with them to visit relatives on the prairies. She wouldn't be able to come either.

Maggie forgave Colleen. She knew that if Colleen had a choice, she would have come. But Maggie would never forgive Uncle Jeff. What was the use in having a charming, fun-loving uncle if every time he had to choose between her and his business, his business came first. Deep in her heart, she knew it would always come first.

Now she was stuck here for a whole month with Aunt Kate, who was Uncle Jeff's aunt as well, which made her Maggie's Great Aunt Kate. Six years ago Aunt Kate had moved into the old family home in Fredericton to help Uncle Jeff care for Maggie when Maggie's mother had died.

Aunt Kate had no interest in wind surfing or horseback riding. Her only interests were bird watching and sleeping in the sun. Aunt Kate seldom laughed. Maggie's eyes began to sting, and she felt terribly sorry for herself.

Aunt Kate grunted and put her straw hat back over her face. She spread her bare arms and legs out on the lounge chair, as if trying to absorb all the warmth of the sun. Soon she was snoring gently.

Maggie sat up and pulled her knees to her chin. She felt a tickle on her bare foot. An ant had climbed from the grass and was crawling up the side of her foot, carrying something in its mouth. She didn't move, but watched it scurry along. It didn't stop once, but when it reached the crest and began the downhill descent on the other side of her foot, she thought it went a little faster. "Whee, halfway home," she said gently, but it didn't pay any attention. Then it disappeared into the grass and she scratched her foot, making little white streaks on the pink skin.

She looked toward the old white farmhouse. The people who owned the cottage that she and Aunt Kate were renting lived there. While the cottage was only forty or fifty metres from the edge of the bank, the house was about a hundred metres farther back on the crest of a hill.

Something moving in front of the farmhouse caught her eye. It was the boy, out in his wheelchair. A basketball was hung on a rope from a tree branch. The boy was using his arm as a bat. He whacked the ball. When it swung back, he whacked it again. He didn't miss very often, but when he did, or when he hit it at an angle so it spun off crazily, he wheeled forward until he was directly under the branch, then he took the ball under his arm and wheeled backward until the rope was taut and used his other arm to bat it.

Maggie noticed that every time he missed the ball, he changed arms. His upper body was tanned and glistening with sweat. He had pulled his tee-shirt off and thrown it on the grass. He wore jeans and sneakers. She knew he had artificial legs. She had seen him walking with two canes. But sometimes, like today, he used his wheelchair instead.

His mother, Mrs. McKay, had brought Maggie and Aunt Kate lemonade and cookies yesterday, after they moved into the cottage. Mrs. McKay drank lemonade with Aunt Kate and told her about her son's automobile accident. His name was Marc and he was twelve, the same age as Maggie.

Maggie thought of him as the boy with no legs. This fact didn't bother her. If anything, it made him a little more interesting than most kids. But she sensed somehow that if she went gushing up to him, trying to be friends, he would think it was because she was sorry for him. Which she was. But she didn't want him to think that. So she pretended she hadn't seen him, and slowly turned her back to him. Then she stood. She tried to brush the grass from her legs and her bathing suit, but she was sweaty and the prickly grass stuck.

"I'm going for a swim, Aunt," she said.

Aunt Kate jerked awake.

"Are you going for a swim this afternoon?" Maggie asked.

Aunt Kate shook her head. "I'm still catching up on my rest. Tomorrow I'll get some exercise."

Maggie ran down the stairs that led from the edge of the bank to the shore. She walked carefully over the rocky beach, taking little steps and big steps so that she walked on only flat stones that would not hurt her feet. She crossed a strip of cool red sand, then more stones at the edge of the water with tangled bits of seaweed caught around them. She waded in, gingerly. The water was icy against her hot skin, so she plunged in, feeling a shocking numbness, then nothing but the pleasure of the coolness and the sharp salt taste on her lips.

She swam out a little way, stopping every few metres to check the depth. About fifty metres out, she could still touch bottom. She relaxed and floated on her back. Then, because the sun made her squeeze her eyes shut, she sat up, her toes peeking above the water in front of her, and the salt water holding her like an easy chair. She could see Aunt Kate, a smaller Aunt Kate now, on a small lawn chair which seemed

9

perched on the edge of the grassy bank. She was still sleeping with her small hat over her face. Behind Aunt Kate was their cottage, and above that, on the hill, was the white house where Marc lived with his parents. She could see the tree where his ball was hanging, but he had disappeared.

She paddled with her left arm until her body swung around in a half-circle. From here she could see the cliffs around the bay. She looked back. The bank in front of their cottage was about five metres high. But most of the bay, what she could see of it, was bordered with red cliffs that were much higher — at least fifteen metres high. In some spots trees grew at the top of the cliffs, a few leaning crazily over the water. She swam lazily to shore.

She was picking her way over the rocks on the beach when she saw the canoe. It was pulled up above dried seaweed that showed the tide line. It was small, just big enough for two. It had two paddles in it and two orange life jackets. There was a little puddle of water in the bottom.

Maggie heard something behind her and swung around to see Marc at the top of the stairs. He was grasping the stair railing with his left hand, and in his right hand was a cane. He stopped on the second step down. He looked startled at seeing her.

"I'm sorry," said Maggie. "Is this your canoe?"

"Yeah. Well, it used to be. My mother and father use it sometimes, and the people in the cottage. That's you now, so you can use it if you want to."

"What do you mean, it used to be yours?"

"Are you blind?" he said, and he flushed a deep scarlet.

Maggie turned hurriedly back to the canoe. "Do you think your parents would mind if I took it for a while?"

"Suit yourself," he said, looking away from her, as if the sea gull circling above the beach was the first one he had ever seen.

She threw one of the paddles and a life jacket onto the bank. Then she pulled on the other life jacket. As she dragged the boat into the water, from the corner of her eye she could see Marc making his slow, painstaking descent down the last three steps and standing alone, staring at her.

Uncle Jeff had taught her how to use a paddle, but it took her a few minutes to get the hang of it again. She pulled to the left, hugging the shoreline. Before she went around a jut of land, she turned and looked back at the boy. He was sitting on the stairs, his head bowed and his hands over his face. With one stroke of her paddle, he disappeared.

The beach changed as she progressed. In some places it was wide and flat, in others only a narrow rocky strip. She heard a small rushing sound and looked up. In the red clay cliff beside her were dozens of tiny round holes. Two small birds flew pell-mell, directly toward the cliff. They each hurtled into a hole. She waited, almost holding her breath, and saw two more. In a moment one flew out again. She pulled around another bit of land. Now she could see the sea more clearly. The sound of the surf was louder and more menacing, and she wondered what made it roar on such a calm day.

Then, above the sound of the surf, she heard another noise. At first it was a hollow, rushing sound, much louder than the birds' wings, then over it she heard the sound of wailing. It sounded like a woman's or a child's voice. And all the time the hollow, rushing sound was there.

Maggie's heart skipped a beat. She raised her paddle, letting it drip carelessly into the canoe as she looked around. There was no one on top of the cliff, at least that she could see. But the sound was closer than that. It was very near.

There was no real beach here, and farther along, the beach was empty. It must be some kind of an illusion, she thought. There were optical illusions, so maybe there were sound illusions as well. But what was different about this spot? The cliffs were higher here, and there were no birds' holes. She could paddle quite close to the cliff, the sound growing louder as she did so. Ah! She could see a difference! This cliff, although it was the same red colour as the others, was made of rock rather than clay.

But that didn't explain the sound that seemed to be all around her now, coming even from beneath her, louder and more echoing. Then the wailing changed. She could hear a voice speaking above the rushing sound. Maggie felt her body go rigid with fear. She grabbed her paddle and began to pull as hard as she could for the cottage, Aunt Kate and safety. The voice followed her. It seemed amplified, as with a microphone. It was saying the same phrase over and over. "*Où est-ce-que vous êtes?*"

The sounds disappeared when she pulled around the first jut of land, but she continued paddling hard until she got to the cottage. She had to drag the boat high up on the beach because the tide had come in. She pulled off the life jacket, jerking at the straps in her hurry, then rushed up the steps, past a startled Aunt Kate, and into the cottage. She ran into her room, slammed the door and dropped on her bed.

Gradually her fear began to drain away as her breathing slowed and her heart stopped pounding. She knew "*Où est-ce-que vous êtes?*" was French for "Where are you?" There must be some explanation for what she had heard, but who could she ask? Not Aunt Kate. She would tell Maggie to stop being foolish. That would be that. Case closed. That's the way Aunt Kate was, and the way she had been ever since Maggie had known her.

She turned to the table by her bed and picked up the framed photograph of her mother. She always kept it by her, even on holidays. She stared into the pretty face with the little smile tugging at the corners of the mouth. Maggie could remember that smile. Her father had died before she was born, and she had no memory of him, but she could remember sitting on her mother's soft lap while she read to her. And she could remember her mother braiding her hair, and the sound of her laughter. Maggie pressed the picture hard against her chest as tears trickled down her cheeks. Maybe the boy had no legs, but at least he had a mother and a father.

Chapter Two

J Dare You!

The next morning Maggie waited until after breakfast to ask Aunt Kate to go canoeing with her. She wanted a witness in case she heard the voice again. They were lingering at the picnic table in front of the cottage, and Aunt Kate was sipping her second cup of coffee.

"Mmmm?" said Aunt Kate, not looking up from her newspaper.

"Please!" said Maggie, a note of desperation in her voice. "You said you wanted to get some exercise today."

"Yes, but I thought a nice walk —"

Maggie remembered that Aunt Kate loved birds, and she had an inspiration. "I saw some birds flying into little holes in the cliff," she said, squinting her eyes a little as she watched for her aunt's reaction.

"Swallows! Yes, it would be nice to go for a little ride. But not until it warms up. Then I'll go for a swim as well."

Maggie knew that now Aunt Kate had made up her mind there was nothing she could do to hurry her. Instead, Maggie helped wash the breakfast dishes, then she and Aunt Kate went out into the sunshine and set up their lawn chairs. Maggie tried to read her book, but she couldn't concentrate. The boy, Marc, was at the tree batting his ball again.

"Why don't you go over and make friends with that poor boy?" asked Aunt Kate.

"I don't think he'd like to be called a poor boy," said Maggie.

"Perhaps not," said Aunt Kate, watching him from under her hat. "But his mother says he's lonely. They're from Hamilton — in Ontario. For years they vacationed in this very cottage. Now they've bought the place and plan to live here year-round. He won't meet many local children until he starts school in the fall."

Maggie remembered how sad the boy looked when he told her the canoe used to be his, and in her mind's eye she could still see him sitting on the steps with his head in his hands.

"Good morning! Another lovely day!" It was Mrs. McKay, Marc's mother, coming toward them. A slim woman, she wore her black hair pulled back into a coil at the nape of her neck. She was wearing a white shirt and lemon-yellow slacks tied at the waist with a black and orange sash. She wore silver hoop earrings and several intricately designed silver rings. Maggie thought she was very beautiful. Maggie got up and sat on the grass near her aunt, offering her chair to their visitor.

"It is lovely here, isn't it?" said Aunt Kate, smiling. Maggie had noticed long ago that Aunt Kate smiled only when she was talking to adults. They looked across the sparkling bay, then at a nearby field where cattle calmly grazed in the gentle sunshine.

"This is what convinced us to give up the rat race in the big city and try to make a living with our pottery and our batiks and tie-dyed fabrics," Mrs. McKay said, fingering her sash.

"You don't mind if we use the canoe, I hope," said Aunt Kate. "I'm afraid my niece has already taken it out."

"Please — whenever you like. John and I are busy in the shop much of the time, and Marc ..." Mrs. McKay's voice trailed off, and her eyes became sad. In a moment she shook her head as if to collect herself and went on. "Marc used to love canoeing and swimming. Swimming in a pool was part of his therapy after the accident, but he refuses to swim now. He feels too self-conscious to wear a bathing suit here, outdoors, where others might see him."

No one said anything for a moment, then Maggie took a deep breath and asked the question that was haunting her.

"Mrs. McKay, are there any French-speaking people living near here?"

"Why do you ask?"

"Oh, I just thought, that is, when I was out in the canoe yesterday, I thought I heard someone calling in French."

"There are French-speaking people on Prince Edward Island, the Acadians." Mrs. McKay laughed. "I'm an Acadian, Maggie. My family's name is Arsenault. My parents were Islanders, but I was born in Ontario, and I'm afraid I've lost the language. One reason we moved back is to get Marc in touch with his heritage. He already speaks French, but John and I want him to know the history and culture of the Acadian people as well. I'm afraid he's not very enthusiastic about that either." She sighed. "But to get back to your question. I suppose there's a possibility that you heard someone — a tourist from Quebec perhaps. And then again —"

"Yes?" said Maggie, leaning forward.

"Do you believe in ghosts?"

"Not really," Maggie answered, grinning.

"Back in the early 1700s, when Prince Edward Island was a colony of France, some Acadian families settled around this bay. They met a very sad fate, I'm afraid. There were many wars in those times between the British and the French. In

1758, when the British got control of the Island, they deported the Acadians. Their soldiers took the French-speaking people from their homes, forced them on ships and sent them across the ocean."

Maggie stopped smiling. "Really? It happened here?"

"Really," said Mrs. McKay grimly. "There's an old story that the ghosts of those early Acadian people return here, to the homes and farms they loved so much." She glanced at her watch. "Oh, look at the time. It's my turn to take over in the shop."

They watched her make her way up the path toward the big house. When she'd disappeared behind a clump of trees, Maggie said, "Whew, it's getting hot!" even though it was only pleasantly warm. She was hoping Aunt Kate would take the hint.

Aunt Kate was glancing through a book about Prince Edward Island. She put it down and shrugged her shoulders. "Oh, all right! Let's go for that canoe ride."

Aunt Kate's paddling was stiff and jerky. They paused a long time near the cliff swallows' nests, then they moved on. They had almost reached the spot where Maggie had heard the voice when a drop of sweat rolled down Aunt Kate's nose and hung on the tip for a moment before she wiped it off with the back of her hand.

"Here's a nice place to beach the canoe," she said. "I vote for a swim."

"Not yet!" Maggie pleaded, but Aunt Kate's vote was the only one that counted.

They beached the canoe. After some gasping and sputtering in the cold water, Aunt Kate was soon swimming lazily, while Maggie sat sullenly on the beach, her paddle in her hand, ready to go. Aunt Kate finally came to shore and sat on a boulder, letting the sun dry her wrinkled, tanned skin.

"See those woods," said Maggie, pointing across the bay. "Do you think there are wild animals there? You know, moose or bears?"

Aunt Kate followed her gaze. "That's only someone's wood-lot," she said. "I read just this morning that the largest wild animal on the Island is the fox — or was it the coyote? The bigger animals were killed off years ago."

They sat quietly for a moment, then Aunt Kate stood up and brushed the dust from the seat of her bathing suit. It was almost lunchtime, time to go back.

Maggie panicked. "Please, Aunt Kate," she begged. "Can't we stay out for just a little longer?" She tried to keep her voice from sounding whiny, because that always made Aunt Kate cross.

"Home, now!" said Aunt Kate sharply. She began pushing the canoe into the water.

Maggie followed. She knew there was no use arguing. When she was small and she begged Aunt Kate for something, her aunt would make a twisting motion by her ears, pretending she had shut them off and couldn't hear. She didn't do that any more, but Maggie felt just as helpless as she used to.

Maggie was so frustrated that when they got to the cottage she locked herself in her room and told her troubles to her mother's picture. Then she closed her eyes tight against a few hot tears while she imagined a soft voice calming her, telling her to be patient, things would work out. But today this old trick didn't work. She still felt angry and helpless. She marched from her room and stood in the hallway a moment, listening to the clink of dishes in the kitchen as Aunt Kate prepared lunch.

She let herself out, careful not to let the screen door bang, and purposefully walked over to the boy who was sitting in his wheelchair under the tree with the ball, doing nothing but gazing over the bay. He looked bored and, when he heard her, annoyed.

"Who are you staring at?" he asked.

Maggie was startled at his rudeness. Did he think he was the only one with troubles? Who did he think he was, anyway, to talk to her like that?

"Didn't your mother teach you any manners?" she asked.

His rudeness quickly turned to anger. "You think you're so smart," he said, "just because you can swim and canoe."

She was stunned for a moment, then all her fears and frustrations seemed to focus on this arrogant boy.

"You make me sick," said Maggie.

Marc looked astonished.

Maggie plunged on. "Just because you had an accident, you've quit doing everything. You just sit around feeling sorry for yourself!"

The boy's face flushed. "Who do you think you are, saying things like that? You've got two legs."

"Sure I do. But you don't and that can't be helped. I know you can swim. Your mother said so. I know you like to canoe. You told me yourself. You could be having fun, but you'd rather sit around doing nothing!"

The boy's face had changed from red to white, and she was afraid he was going to cry. But she'd gone too far to turn back now.

"I'm going out this afternoon to explore the bay some more. At two o'clock." She grabbed this time out of the air. "I dare you to come with me."

He stared at her. His mouth opened but nothing came out.

"I dare you!" Maggie repeated, but in a smaller voice now, because she was starting to wonder just what she was doing.

She turned away and marched quickly back to the cottage, her heart pounding, not sure whether she had just done a terrible thing or not.

Chapter Three

A Picture of the Past

Mrs. McKay guided her old station wagon down the road, all the while managing to carry on a lively conversation with Aunt Kate. They were talking about Toronto. Aunt Kate told her that she had worked there for years as a clerk at Eaton's department store. But when her nephew's widow died in Fredericton leaving a six-year-old daughter, Aunt Kate moved back to the family home to help her other nephew raise the child.

"I gave up an independent life," she said grimly. "But the child needs me."

In the back seat Maggie stared resolutely out the window at passing fields. She had heard Aunt Kate's story many times. It always made her feel lonely and lost. In a field she saw one horse nip another, then both kicked up their heels and galloped around their pasture. She saw neat farmsteads behind white fences, and bits of blue sea sparkling between green hills. Fields of grain waved at her. Other fields were filled with rows of potato plants, marching like little green soldiers across the slopes.

The land began to change. It became flatter and the roadside was lined with bushes and scrubby trees. Now she saw flags flying by almost every house. The flags were red, white and blue with a yellow star in the corner. Mrs. McKay said they were the flag of the Acadian people. All the while, Maggie kept her back to Marc, who was just as busy staring out his window. They didn't speak a word to each other.

At two o'clock that afternoon Maggie had been sitting on the beach by the canoe as she said she would be, waiting, half-hoping Marc would show up, and yet half-scared that he would. When she heard someone approaching, she looked up, only to see Aunt Kate beckoning, telling her to hurry. Mrs. McKay was taking the afternoon off and had invited them for a drive to the western part of Prince Edward Island where most Acadians lived. Now Maggie was stuck here in the back seat with Marc.

Their first stop was at a little fishing village where Mrs. McKay's aunt, Tante Helen, lived. Marc seemed to cheer up at the prospect of seeing her. With his canes and his stiff gait, he walked ahead of Maggie to the side door of a pretty house painted a shiny blue. Without knocking, he went into his great-aunt's kitchen. Maggie followed.

The window blinds were pulled against the heat of the July afternoon, and Maggie had to wait a minute until her eyes adjusted to the gloom. She heard Aunt Kate and Mrs. McKay enter the kitchen just as a large woman wearing a white blouse, gray cotton pants and a black and white striped apron, came into the room from another door. Her gray hair curled around her shiny face. This must be Tante Helen. When she saw who her visitors were, her eyes crinkled with happiness.

"Adele!" she cried, giving Marc's mother a hug. She ruffled Marc's hair and he grinned. When Maggie and Aunt Kate were introduced, she insisted they all stay for a cup of tea. She bustled about, and by the time they sat down for their tea, she also had plates of sandwiches, homemade pickles and large squares of chocolate cake on her kitchen table.

When they had finished eating, the adults sat back for a second cup of tea and more conversation. Marc asked to be excused.

"Take your friend into the front room and show her the pictures of your uncle," his aunt said.

Marc looked a little embarrassed but he and Maggie made their escape.

In the front room, on top of the TV, was a framed photograph of a fisherman hauling a lobster trap out of the ocean onto the deck of his boat. His face was turned toward the camera, and he was smiling broadly.

"That's Uncle Paul," said Marc. "He died last year, but he used to be a fisherman. Aunt Helen likes that picture best."

"Earlier you called her Tante Helen," said Maggie." I thought your relatives were French, but you're all talking English."

"Acadian," Marc corrected. "French people live in France. My mother's family is Acadian. My aunt's speaking English because Mom doesn't remember much French and because you and your aunt are here and you wouldn't understand."

"Oh, yes, I would. I'm in French immersion at school."

Marc looked surprised. "How old are you? What grade are you in?" he asked.

"I'm twelve now. I'm going into grade eight in the fall."

"I thought you were younger," he said with his old surliness, "because you're so short and skinny."

Maggie felt like shooting back a rude remark, but she remembered that his mother and Aunt Kate were in the next room and decided to hold her tongue.

"What grade are you in?" she asked, trying to be polite, but his manner had so annoyed her that the words came our harshly.

"Going into seven — French immersion, too. I'm twelve already, though. I missed a grade when I had my accident." He said this quite naturally, which surprised her. Before he had seemed so self-conscious.

"Look, I know you don't like me —" he began.

"It's not that I don't like —" she said quickly, but he interrupted.

"And I don't like you much either. But we're stuck with each other for the rest of the day. Truce?"

Maybe he is a spoiled baby, she thought, but at least he's honest. "Truce," she said at last.

"What's all this stuff?" asked Maggie. She picked up a scrapbook from a stack on the sideboard.

"Oh, that's Tante Helen's history," said Marc. "She's been interviewing old people for years and writing down their stories. Usually when we come here, Mom asks her to read us one of the stories. Some of them are about things that happened a couple of hundred years ago — at least that's what Tante Helen says. But I don't really believe it. Nothing was written down in those times, and if a story was told as many times as they say, from one generation to the next, it would get all mixed up and changed. But Tante Helen believes all this old junk really happened."

Maggie began to read one of the typewritten stories in the scrapbook. She read French well, but she couldn't understand some of the words. "What does *juyette* mean?"

"That's the Acadian way of saying *juillet* — July," he said. "They still use some words that haven't been used anywhere else for a couple of hundred years. And I think they've created some words of their own. I don't understand them all either."

Maggie skimmed over the parts she couldn't understand, but she could make out the gist of the story. It happened before the deportation in the 1700s. A boy and girl from a settlement had wandered into the woods one day and were never seen again. They had probably been killed by the wild animals that lived in the terrible forest. It was hard to imagine this gentle green island ever being so dark and dangerous. Maggie shivered.

Before Maggie could comment on the story, Marc's mother appeared in the doorway and said they would have to leave now if they wanted to stop at the museum in Miscouche on their way home. Maggie followed the others to the car. She looked once more toward the pretty blue house before crawling into the back seat.

When they arrived at the Acadian Museum, Marc petulantly insisted on waiting in the car while the others went in. Maggie was therefore surprised when he joined her in front of a mural depicting the deportation.

They were alone. They stood in silence for a few moments, staring at the painting of families dressed in the traditional Acadian clothing of the eighteenth century. The people clung together on the shore while ships waited in the harbour to take them away across the ocean. Soldiers with guns lurked in the background. It was a heart-wrenching scene. Maggie wanted to show that she was sorry that these terrible things had happened to Marc's ancestors, but she didn't know how to say it. Marc turned away and went back to the car.

On the way home, Marc was quiet.

"Mrs. McKay," said Maggie, "you said the Acadians who lived around the bay met a sad fate. That picture in the museum made me realize how terrible it was."

"It seems especially hard," said Mrs. McKay, "when you remember that it was the second expulsion. Some people had escaped the first deportation to come here, to Prince Edward Island, where they thought they would be safe."

"But they weren't," said Maggie.

"No, they weren't," said Mrs. McKay quietly.

The car tires hummed on the road. Maggie's eyes grew heavy and her head nodded.

Mrs. McKay stopped the car near the cottage. Just as Maggie was opening her door, Marc leaned over and said in her ear, "Two o'clock tomorrow. I promise!"

Chapter Four

The Voice in the Storm

A gust of wind ruffled Maggie's hair as she tied one of the life jackets over her sweatshirt. She had on her bathing suit, but she wearing jeans and a sweat-shirt over it. The breeze was cool. She glanced anxiously at the sky just as the cloud that had hovered overhead for the last few minutes parted and the sun broke through.

"Hi, Maggie!" a deep voice shouted. She looked to the top of the bank to see a man who carried Marc on his back. He walked carefully down the stairs, then deposited Marc in the canoe.

"I'm John McKay, Marc's father," the man said, shaking Maggie's hand. He had blue eyes and a shaggy red-gray beard. "I'm beginning to wonder if you kids should be going out," he said, squinting at the sky. "If the wind comes up, it could get dangerous."

Maggie's heart sank. "We'll be careful," she said quickly.

"All right, but you stick close to the shore," he said, "and promise to come right back if the weather starts acting up."

"Sure, Dad," said Marc in an embarrassed voice. "We're not little kids, you know."

"We'll be careful," said Maggie. "I have my badge in water safety."

"We're not going to cross the Atlantic," Marc added.

Mr. McKay helped Maggie launch the canoe, then waded back to shore, his sneakers squelching water.

"Don't go too far," he shouted as they pulled away.

"Parents," said Marc from his position behind her. "I had an awful time getting away. He wanted me to help weed the garden." Marc said this in a how-stupid-can-you-get tone of voice.

Maggie glanced at him over her shoulder. He had his life jacket on over an old shirt and rolled-up jeans. Maggie couldn't help looking at one pant leg that had come unrolled and flopped on the floor in front of Marc's seat. He flushed a little.

"I can't wear my legs in a boat because if we swamp, I couldn't swim with them on."

"Makes sense to me," said Maggie nonchalantly. "Have you been along the edge of the bay lately?"

"Not for a couple of years. Why?"

"Do you remember seeing anything mysterious? Or hearing anything?"

"No." He looked puzzled.

She began paddling. It took a few minutes for Marc to find a comfortable position, then he fell in with her rhythm. The canoe glided easily and quickly. She looked back a couple of times. His face had a light sheen of sweat from his effort. He had changed his position again so that his weight rested on his right haunch while his left leg, the longer one, which extended to just below the knee, was propped against the floor of the canoe.

"If I sit this way, I can get some leverage," he explained.

"Maybe we shouldn't go too far until you get used to it."

"I'm okay!" he said belligerently. "If I need any special consideration, I'll let you know."

Oh, oh, thought Maggie, the bad-mood blues again. But she didn't say anything. In a few moments she felt little side-to-side movements in the canoe and realized he was shifting his weight. They were near the point of land behind which she had heard the voice. She was anxious to go on, but they had come a long way very quickly, and she was afraid he might become exhausted.

"Let's take a break," she called, pulling up her paddle. He didn't argue, and they floated, not speaking.

They were close to the spot where she and Aunt Kate had stopped yesterday, but the beach was narrower now because the tide was coming in. The sun disappeared again as clouds rolled over them and a strong gust of wind ruffled the water. The canoe bobbed up and down.

"Maybe we should turn back," said Marc. "Dad'll be watching for us. He'll never let me out again if we don't do what he said."

"Could we go just a bit farther?" asked Maggie. "There's something around this point I want to show you. It'll just take a minute." A drop of rain hit her cheek as she spoke.

"Okay by me," said Marc. "It's not like I'm tired or anything. Let's go." He dug his paddle into the water and pulled with such force that Maggie almost lost her balance.

As they rounded the point, the rain plastered bits of Maggie's long hair across her face. The waves were getting higher, and they stayed close to the cliffs. Maggie had just decided that they had better turn back when she heard the rushing sound, then the wailing. It was the voice she had heard before, a woman's or a child's crying as if in a torment of grief. It began almost inaudibly, masked by the other sounds, then it built and grew until it seemed to be coming from all around them. "Oo-ooooo, *où est-ce-que vous êtes?*"

Maggie looked back at Marc. His paddle was on the floor of the canoe, and he was holding the sides as the light craft rocked on the rising waves. He didn't look frightened, but he was listening hard, his forehead wrinkled and his head turned to one side.

"What is it?" Maggie shouted above the sound of the wailing and the strengthening wind. But before Marc could answer, Maggie screamed and pointed in the direction of the ocean. Several waves were rolling toward them, seeming to grow as they came. And behind them rushed a monster wave, pushing smaller waves before it.

Marc swung his head and looked just as the first wave hit. Maggie dropped her paddle and grabbed the sides of the canoe. It rocked dangerously. Then the following waves hit. She felt as if she was being pushed back by a giant arm, something so powerful that she couldn't struggle against it. Then she was in the water.

The waves swept over her. When she could see again, the canoe was bobbing upside down in front of her. She reached out, but her hand glanced off the canoe's smooth side and the boat skittered away. Another wave swept over her. She came up sputtering, a terrible taste of salt in her mouth and throat. It was raining hard now, and she couldn't see Marc.

"Marc," she tried to shout, but the effort made her cough and her voice was lost in the sounds of the wind and the sea. She knew she had to reach the canoe. The life jacket was holding her upright. She let her body relax against it, then pulled up one knee then the other and tugged off her sneakers. She took another gasp of air and hung in the water while she unzipped her jeans. It took a minute of pulling and kicking before the heavy, water-soaked pants finally came free. Then she swam toward the canoe, a few metres away. It seemed to be moving crazily, first one direction, then another. At last she reached it.

The first time she touched it, it slipped away, but on the second attempt she managed to get a grip on its rim. With her other hand she reached for the ridge that ran the length of the canoe. Finally she caught it with her fingers. She rested her head against the side of the frail little craft, feeling gasps of air rush in and out of her lungs as she and the canoe rose and fell on the waves.

"Maggie!" It was Marc yelling. She could see his orange life jacket bobbing about ten metres out in the bay.

"Over here!" she shouted.

"I can't," he yelled. Then his voice was cut off. When she could hear again, he was shouting, "… can't get anywhere."

Maggie remembered how hard Marc had been paddling. She was afraid he wouldn't have the strength to save himself.

"Your jeans," she shouted, then waited for a lull. "Take them off!"

When she looked again, the orange life jacket was moving toward her, slowly and unsteadily. "The other side," she yelled. "Get on the other side of the canoe."

It took some minutes of manoeuvring, and several times Maggie was afraid that she was going to lose the canoe, but finally Marc was able to position himself across from her. They grasped wrists across the boat and struggled to recover their breath.

Suddenly Maggie realized that the canoe was moving in one direction now. She felt her body being dragged through the water.

"We're being taken out to sea!" Maggie yelled, panic in her voice.

"I don't think so," answered Marc. "The tide's coming in."

Maggie knew he was right. But something strange was going on. Even though the waves were washing toward shore, the canoe was slicing through them and heading obliquely toward the cliffs. Each wave washed over Maggie and Marc, leaving them sputtering, but still, miraculously, hanging on. Soon their hands were numb with cold and strain. They were still moving very fast. Maggie looked up at the sharp crags above them. The canoe was pulling them toward the cliffs. She was terrified that they would crash, but to free herself from the canoe, she had to let go of Marc.

She did what she had to do. She let go. She could feel the tight pressure of his fingers sliding from her wrists.

She was swamped by a wave. She felt the canoe scrape hard against her arm, then it was gone. She swam a few strokes, then reached up and grabbed a rocky ledge. She tried to get a foothold, but it was impossible. The cliff was sheer. She clung to her fingerhold and looked, but both Marc and the canoe had disappeared.

"Marc!" she screamed, but her scream was swallowed by the roaring sound all around her.

She scrambled and clawed with her free arm for a second grip. Water washed over and she couldn't see, but her hand caught something, was pulled away, then caught it again. She could fold her right hand around an edge of rock. She pulled herself toward it. But this movement meant she had to let go with her left hand. As she moved, she was caught by the force in the water once more, and she was swept helplessly along the cliffs. She screwed her eyes shut, waiting for impact. But it didn't come.

Instead of feeling the sharp surface of rock, she felt herself hurtling at great speed within a rush of water. In her mind was a soundless scream. She was being whirled along by some ferocious watery force.

Suddenly it was over. The force was gone, and the noise was muffled and faraway. She was floating, face up. She opened her eyes and saw a rock ceiling shimmering in pale, water-reflected light. Then she heard a gentle lapping sound. Each lap was followed by a small echo, so it sounded *LAP-lap, LAP-lap*. It was as soft and peaceful a sound as the roaring had been terrifying. She realized she was in a cave. She breathed deeply, closed her eyes and rested.

After a moment she began to shake. Deep sobs rolled from her body as she cried, "Marc, Marc."

Chapter Five

Escape from the Cave

"Here I am!"

Maggie looked up and behind her, toward the sound of the voice. Marc sat on a narrow ledge about half a metre above the water line. She swam over and tried to jump up beside him, but she was tired and missed on the first try. He reached down, grabbed her life jacket and hoisted as she jumped. This time she made it.

"I thought you had drowned," she gasped.

"I almost did. I was afraid I was going to be carried out to sea. How did we get in here, anyway?"

They looked for an opening in the wall of the cave but could see nothing.

"The tide was coming in. The entrance is probably below the water line now," said Maggie. "All we have to do is wait for the tide to go out. Then we can get out."

The cave seemed small. When she imagined furniture in it,

she decided it must be about the same size as the living room in her home in Fredericton. Because of the water, she had no idea how high it was, but the ceiling was about three metres above the ledge.

"Where is the light coming from?" asked Mark.

They scanned the walls and ceiling but could see no opening.

"There's nothing we can do but wait for the tide to go out. Then we'll swim out the opening," Maggie said. "I think the storm's already dying down."

They listened. The roar of the sea was even fainter and farther away than before.

"Yeah, there's nothing to worry about," said Marc, but there was a note of doubt in his voice.

They let their bodies slump against the rock wall. Since Maggie felt weak and tired and her legs ached, she lay down on the narrow ledge.

She yawned. "Everything will be okay soon." Her hand dropped over the side of the ledge but she was too tired to pull it up. She slept for perhaps five or ten minutes, then something awakened her. She was cold, the ledge was hard, and she was afraid to shift her body for fear of falling. But that wasn't what had wakened her. At first she wasn't sure what it was, then she felt something cold on the hand that was hanging over the ledge. It was water!

"Marc." She tried to speak calmly. "Marc, the water's rising."

Marc was alert in an instant. They looked up. Above them there was just rock wall, no other ledges. The water inexorably crept up. As it rose above the ledge, Maggie stood up with her back to the wall and sidestepped close to Marc. He reached up and took her hand. And still the water rose. They waited silently, their hearts beating wildly.

Maggie couldn't stand it any longer. "Let's get busy and find a way out." She jumped into the water and Marc followed. They paddled wildly around the perimeter of the cave, Maggie going one way, Marc the other, searching for an opening. They took gulps of air and swam underwater. All they found were solid rock walls.

"Oh, Marc!" Maggie said when they'd completed their search. She felt she might start to cry again.

"Something weird's going on here," Marc said. "Where is all this light coming from?"

With something to concentrate on, Maggie felt calmer. "What a strange light!" she said. "It's greenish — eerie!"

They began exploring the rock ceiling, now within reach. Maggie let her hand run across its surface, searching for a crack.

"It's no use," Marc floated on his back, eyes closed. His face was tinged an awful pale green by the light that was all around them. It was stronger, Maggie was sure, than it had been moments before.

Strange, she didn't feel frightened now. They were both facing death once again, certain that there was no escape, and she felt nothing but the serenity of the rising water gently lapping against the rock walls. Perhaps she was suffering from a kind of mental paralysis caused by the terror of the storm. She, too, floated on her back and shut her eyes. The water was so gentle, so quiet, and she rocked slightly, relaxed and sleepy.

Her face touched something cold for a moment, and her eyes flew open. She was only centimetres from the ceiling and a ripple had lifted her head so her face had touched it. Soon there would be no place left to breathe.

"Maggie," Marc said, his voice quivering. Then she felt his hand, his fingers biting into hers.

"My dad will kill me if we ever get out of this," he said. Then he laughed, a high-pitched scared laugh that was suddenly cut off when his face bobbed against the ceiling.

"Marc," Maggie said quietly, "I'm glad you're with me. I mean, I'm sorry we're here, but I'm glad I'm not alone."

Marc didn't answer, but she felt his hand squeezing hers again. Then something happened that made them hang onto the other's hand with all their strength. They began floating in a circle, slowly at first, then faster and faster. The ceiling was whirling. Maggie felt dizzy. She screwed her eyes shut. A great rushing sound filled her ears. She didn't know whether she and Marc were screaming; she knew only that they were whirling as if in a cyclone.

Then it stopped.

For a moment Maggie lay completely still, then she carefully moved her shoulder. It scraped against something hard. She shifted her weight. She was on something solid and uneven. She opened her eyes and gazed up. Above her were thickly interlocking tree branches and bits of sky.

She sat up, full of wonder. Marc was sitting beside her, gazing around in amazement. They were on a forest floor, and the light around them had a greenish tinge, stained by the leaves around and above them. At their backs was a giant pine tree. Maggie looked up. The top of the tree thrust into the sky, far above all the trees around it.

At the base of the tree was a hole as big around as a dining-room table. She lay on her stomach and looked into it. Beside her Marc also stretched out and peered into its depths. For a moment they could see only blackness. Then they saw something glitter a couple of metres down. It was light reflecting off water. The water was swirling in a circle. They heard a faraway voice, and they turned from the hole to listen, but the call floated on the still air, then was gone.

Maggie looked down at herself. First, she examined a bloody scratch that ran from her bare knee to her ankle. Then she realized her life jacket was gone and she was no longer wearing her bathing suit and sweatshirt. She was clothed in a kind of plain shirt that reached below her knees and was made of cream-coloured cloth with brown flecks in it. It was smudged with soil and had small tears in it. She touched it, puzzled. It was dry, absolutely dry. She looked at Marc. He was dressed only in pants made of the same light-coloured cloth. And, even more amazing, his face was dirty. How could this be? But Marc was staring at his feet.

His feet! She realized then, as if her mind was in slow motion and could take in these incomprehensible events only one at a time, that Marc had both his legs!

Before she could speak, she heard voices shouting in the distance. The words were slow and came at measured intervals. It was a moment before she could make them out.

"Marguerite! Jean-Marc! Marguerite! Jean-Marc!" The words were repeated over and over again. Then a woman's voice alone, a voice full of fear and sorrow, "Marguerite! Jean-Marc! *Où est-ce-que vous êtes?*"

Chapter Six

Bear!

Marc and Maggie sat perfectly still, listening to the voices and the sound of branches cracking in the forest. In a moment a hat appeared as a man entered the clearing with his head down, protecting his face from the branches he pushed his way through. He raised his head and saw the children. The words froze on his lips. For a second he was immobile, then he rushed toward them, shouting, "*Les enfants! Les enfants!*" Marc reached for Maggie's hand and they clung to each other.

Then everything got confusing. After much crashing through the undergrowth, several men, all talking at once, surrounded them. The first man was carrying a rifle, but the others carried only long sticks. One, shorter than the others, with much gray in his beard, swept Marc into his arms and clasped him in a giant hug.

"Jean-Marc! My son! My son!" he repeated in French, over and over. A few tears squeezed between his tightly shut eyelids.

"Marguerite!" a woman shouted, pushing past the men and bending over Maggie. "Are you hurt?" She reached out and touched Maggie's shoulder. Maggie shook her head. She didn't speak. The woman fell on her knees beside her, pulled Maggie's head to her chest, and sobbed and laughed at the same time. She was dressed in a striped skirt, a white blouse and apron and a small white cap that tied beneath her chin. Even more strange to Maggie's eyes, these people were wearing wooden shoes.

For a moment Maggie thought she and Marc must be at the Acadian Museum for this woman was dressed much like the figures in the mural depicting the deportation. Perhaps the cave they had been trapped in backed onto the museum, and they were in the middle of some sort of historical recreation. But that was impossible. The museum was miles from the bay.

The people were still talking all at once and laughing. The French they spoke sounded strange. The accent was different from any Maggie had heard before, and some of the words puzzled her.

The short man took Marc's arm and began leading him away. Marc looked over his shoulder and caught Maggie's eye. He drew the back of his hand slowly across his mouth. She understood. They must not speak. They were being mistaken for two other children. They must not be discovered as imposters, at least not until they knew what was going on.

They all began walking through the forest on a trail that ran beside a stream. Marc was near the front of the group. Maggie studied the five men walking in single file in front of her, and the woman beside her, holding her hand. Each man's clothes were a little different in cut and condition from the others', but all were of the same rough cloth. They all wore gray shirts and dark pants; one wore a leather vest, and they all wore hats pulled down to their eyebrows, giving them a menacing look. But these men were too cheerful and talkative to be frightening. And the quiet woman held Maggie's hand gently. Maggie was rather surprised that she didn't feel in the least scared. Not scared, just interested in what was going to happen next.

Their progress was slowed by roots and fallen trees that blocked their path. The trees at the side of the trail were bigger than any Maggie had ever seen. She tried to imagine putting her arms around one and hugging it the way she hugged the big old elm in front of the house in Fredericton. As far as she could tell, it would take two people to reach around one of these trees, one on each side.

The talking and laughing continued. Maggie gathered that the children she and Marc were being mistaken for had been missing for nearly three days. Now that these people believed they had found them, everyone was in great spirits.

The woman helped her over logs and fallen branches. Maggie stumbled and gasped as she scraped her bare foot on a root protruding from the ground. The woman called to one of the men who stepped off the path and waited until they came up beside him, then he swung Maggie into his arms and carried her. The woman walked beside them, her hand on Maggie's bleeding foot.

They came to a spring gushing from the ground. Half a small hollowed log had been inserted into the mouth of the spring. The other end of the log was propped up a half-metre or so off the ground. The water from the spring ran along the half-log and fell to the ground below. The area where the water landed and trickled away was covered with stones. The air smelled moist and fresh and cool.

"La Source," said the woman. "We are near home." She smiled.

The path became wider now and more worn. The man carrying Maggie put her down, and she walked with the woman holding her hand. Soon they came to a meadow that lay in a long strip between the forest and the shore of a bay. It looked like the bay that Maggie and Marc had been canoeing on, but instead of green fields and tiny woodlots, this bay was surrounded by dark forests. Only this one strip of meadow was clear.

Maggie counted six log cabins in a line along the meadow, all situated well back from the water. Each was separated from its neighbour by plots of wild grass and vegetable gardens. Each cabin had a crude shed or barn beside or in front of it. Fields of grain and other crops stretched in front of the buildings down to the shore. Stumps of trees showed where the forest had been pushed back in the area behind the cabins.

The man walking with Marc gave a loud cry, and heads popped out of doorways. People waved from fields and shouted, happy that the children had been found. The group dispersed then; Marc went with this man who called him his son into the first cabin they came to.

The woman led Maggie past the cabin in which Marc had disappeared, along a path that stretched between patches of vegetables, then along a fence made of tangled branches and tree roots. The fence formed a kind of corral. The door of a shed opened into the corral, but the doorway was too dark for Maggie to see what was inside. Just beyond the corral was another log cabin.

The woman pushed open the door of this cabin and, slipping out of her wooden shoes in the doorway, led Maggie inside. The light was so dim that Maggie could see nothing for the moment except two tiny windows, one in the front wall, the other in the back. Next she saw flames flickering in a fireplace at the end of the room, and she smelled traces of smoke in the hot air. Gradually her eyes adjusted to the gloom. In the middle of the floor was a long table, and on either side of it were benches.

Maggie sat on a bench, and the woman brought a bowl of cool water and began bathing her face, her hands, the scratch on her leg, then her hurt foot. The cloth felt good on her hot skin, and the woman's touch was gentle.

"My poor child," she murmured as she worked. "Why are you in your chemise? What happened to your clothes, little one? Was it a wild animal? Not a bear?" She peered closely into Maggie's face but Maggie said nothing. The woman had serious, dark eyes.

A simmering pot hung over the fire. At either side of the fireplace was a chair, one of them a rocking chair. Beside the straight-backed chair was a spinning wheel. At the end of the room opposite the fireplace was a bed with a wooden box at its foot.

The woman wiped Maggie's hair back from her forehead with the cloth, then led her to another bed, built along the back wall. Maggie crawled in, and the woman pulled a light blanket over her. It was made of the same itchy cloth as her shirt. Maggie's muscles were aching from her struggles in the water and the long walk through the forest. She snuggled down. The sweet-smelling mattress made a rustling sound. It must be stuffed with straw, she thought, as she fell into an exhausted sleep.

It seemed that hours had passed when she woke, but there was still light at the windows. She had been wakened by voices outside, high and excited. Several people entered the cabin and filed quietly to the side of her bed.

"We searched miles to the west," she heard a man's voice say. "Jean-Baptiste and his boys went east."

"But we found them," said the woman, her voice trembling a little. "We brought them home." She turned to Maggie. "We would have searched the whole of Île St. Jean if necessary to find you!" When the woman said, "The whole of Île St. Jean," Maggie felt that she meant the whole world.

The man bent forward and put his hand on Maggie's head. His voice was husky with emotion, but there were deep crinkles around his eyes, as if he was usually smiling. He had a spiky black beard, and tufts of wiry black hair jutted out from his head, giving him the look of an unruly but friendly bear.

"You are well, Marguerite?" When she didn't answer he looked up at the woman.

"Neither child has spoken," she said. "Not once since we found them."

"They have had a fright," he said. "I have seen it before — this loss of speech after an ordeal. They must rest."

He stepped aside and motioned the boys behind him to come forward. There were four, ranging in age from about eight to fourteen or fifteen. They came forward, one at a time. "Good day, Marguerite," each said formally, except for the biggest who said, "Good day, little one."

Two little girls scrambled up behind the boys. Their brown eyes were large and shy, and they held their hands over their mouths as if trying to hide their smiles. The littler one seemed to be trying to suppress a laugh and a couple of little chirps emanated from behind her hand. She reminded Maggie of a bird.

"Come away from your sister. The supper is ready," said the woman firmly. The family gathered around the table, but before they sat they asked a blessing on their food. The woman brought Maggie a bowl of pea soup and a chunk of bread. The soup was hot and thick. The bread was made of coarsely ground grain. It took a lot of chewing but it was moist and fresh.

"May I have more bread?" asked the youngest girl.

The woman looked sharply at the man. The other children kept their eyes downcast; not a spoon was raised.

"You will have more tomorrow," the woman said brightly.

When she had finished eating, Maggie lay back, a languorous weakness bathing her body. She wasn't frightened, but she was puzzled. "Home," the woman had said. "We brought them home." When she thought of home, she thought of the big house on George Street in Fredericton, but these people, in this rough little cabin, believed they had brought her home. How could this be?

These strangely dressed people called her Marguerite. This Marguerite was apparently the sister of the other children. How could they possibly confuse her with a member of the family? She searched her mind for an explanation, but could fine none. Part of her wanted to get up and march out. She would find Marc and they would go home. But she remembered the look in his eyes when he had signalled her to be quiet. He had been pleading with her. She decided to wait and watch. Surely it wouldn't take long to figure things out.

When they finished eating, the family prayed again, then the man and the boys went outside, saying they would bring the animals in from the meadow and lock them up for the night. The woman gave the little girls a basin of warm water, and they began washing and wiping dry the tin plates and cups and the wooden bowls. The woman talked to them as she swept the crumbs from beneath the table with a broom made of twigs and branches. The name of the bigger girl, who was perhaps six years old, was Jeanne, and the smaller, a year or two younger, was Françoise. When they finished, they poured the dishwater into a bucket by the door. Maggie let her hand drop to the floor. It was cool, hard-packed earth.

When the man and his sons returned, the cabin was tidy and the few dishes had been stacked neatly on a shelf on the wall. There were more prayers. Maggie was not a Catholic, but she realized these people were, and she watched carefully as they held their hands in prayer, made the sign of the cross and addressed a small carved statue of the Virgin Mary, which was kept in a place of honour on its own tiny shelf. Beside the statue were some dried flowers in a wooden bowl and two candles.

After prayers the four boys bowed slightly to their parents, then in single file climbed a ladder at the head of Maggie's bed into an upstairs room. They lowered a trap door over the opening. She could hear their feet on the floor and the murmurs of their voices. The two little girls removed their blouses and striped skirts. Dressed now like Maggie, in long shirts, they crawled into bed, one on each side with Maggie in the middle. They twisted and turned a little, but soon they were still, breathing evenly in sleep.

The noises from upstairs quietened. The man and woman sat in the chairs by the fire, which had died down. Only one candle flickered, but Maggie could see their movements. The man whittled, his knife sending slivers spinning to the floor. Occasionally he paused, laid the knife on his knee and puffed his pipe. The woman knitted without ceasing, her hands moving rhythmically.

They spoke so quietly Maggie had to hold her breath to hear them. Although there were words she couldn't understand, like dropped stitches in a piece of knitting, she could make out that they were discussing Marguerite and Jean-Marc. She heard the words, *la peur, l'ours* and *la Sainte Vierge*, which she knew meant fear, bear, and the Holy Virgin.

"The children must rest," the man said. "The others will do their tasks until they are well."

Maggie lay awake a long time, trying to understand what had happened. She listened to the soft voices and the sound of the woman's rocking chair — *creak, creak* — comforting as a lullaby. She turned on her side, dodging the knobby elbows of the little girls. She was confused, but she felt safe in this snug little cabin. She was sure that she and Marc would go home soon. In the meantime, she would consider this an interesting adventure. The last thing she heard before she fell asleep was the sound of an owl hooting far away in the wild forest.

In the morning there were prayers again. The woman asked Maggie how she was, and when Maggie didn't answer, she helped her dress. Maggie's outfit was like the woman's. Her red and blue striped skirt came almost to her ankles. She was barefoot. The woman smoothed Maggie's long brown hair back from her face, then placed a small white cap on her head and tied it under her chin.

The woman prepared breakfast of boiled grains, which she served with molasses and milk. The family ate at the table, but the woman insisted that Maggie sit by the fireplace where her food was brought to her as if she was an invalid. After breakfast, everyone except Maggie went to work. Maggie could hear the boys, so quiet and formal indoors, shouting and teasing each other as they walked from the cabin to the fields. She could hear the rhythmic whacks of an axe and knew someone was cutting down a tree.

The little girls washed the breakfast dishes while the woman carefully scraped the last bits of boiled grain from the pot into the bucket by the door. Then the woman placed the pot outside the door, telling the girls to go to the shore and get some sand to scrub it while she milked Isabelle.

"Poor Isabelle," she said. "She is mooing because it is getting late and she is uncomfortable with her udder so full." At least, that's what Maggie thought she was saying.

When she was alone, Maggie rose from her chair. How she longed to leave the stuffy cabin and join the children at the shore! But she had made up her mind to continue the pretence that she was ill until she could meet with Marc and plan their return home. She wondered if he would blame her for getting them into this strange place. If only she hadn't dared him into going out on the bay!

Maggie sighed. Her skin itched under her heavy clothing. Flies buzzed in the heavy air. She wandered aimlessly around the small room letting her fingertips trail across the table top, the chair backs, the bed posts. The furniture was roughly made, with nicks and gouges of axe and knife clearly visible.

She needed something to do. She wanted to read. She looked everywhere, but there was not one printed word in the cabin. Nor was there anything, she realized suddenly, beyond the most basic necessities of living. There were no ornaments, no pictures, only the simple statue of the Virgin watching over the home from its rough-hewn shelf.

The children called their parents Maman and Papa. She liked the man's ready smile and cheerful whistle. She couldn't help smiling when he got excited and ran his hands through his hair making it stand on end! She wouldn't mind calling him Papa, because she had no memory of her father. She liked the woman, too, with her eyes so kind and patient, but it didn't feel right to call her Maman, not when Maggie thought about her own mother. She would think of this woman as Madame.

Maggie looked out the front window. In the fields people were hoeing, their backs nearly parallel with the ground. A few scrawny chickens tottered around the stumps and scratched for bugs. Near the corral, the little girls were hard at work scrubbing the pot. Madame came back toward the house. Maggie had just enough time to scurry to the chair beside the fireplace before the woman came in to get the bucket which stood by the door. Maggie again watched from the window as Madame moved toward the shed, one arm out to balance the heavy wooden bucket.

Madame entered the corral, which was attached to the shed, then she spilled the contents of the bucket into a wooden trough. As if listening for the sound of its breakfast, a lean pig with a pink belly trotted from the shed into the enclosure and began an enthusiastic sloshing and eating, grunting loudly as he buried his snout in the watery mixture. Maggie realized that even dishwater would have some nourishment in it from the grease and fragments of food washed from the dishes. Madame picked up a stick and used it to scratch behind the pig's ears. Then she went into the shed.

In a few minutes she came out carrying another bucket. In the other hand she held the ends of two ropes that were attached to a red and white cow and a red calf. She led them to a grassy patch, tied them up and left them to graze.

Maggie heard a rustling behind her and turned back into the dim room. The sound was more a scratching than a rustling. The room seemed even darker than usual. Then she saw that something was blocking the light from the back window. A huge, black, furry paw was scraping across the window as if searching for a crack, a place to pry open. A head appeared, and in an instant she realized it was the head of a bear. It turned so that one of its eyes was at the window.

Maggie froze; her mouth opened to scream but then she realized, almost at once, that even if the bear broke the window, it couldn't fit through the small opening. She felt very excited. "A real live bear!" she said.

It blinked lazily. It's not afraid of me, she thought, then she realized that it couldn't see her inside the dark cabin. She heard someone yell. Probably someone in the fields had spotted the bear. Startled, it pulled its head back, then swung down to its four feet. She ran to the window, frightened for the people outside. She was just in time to see the bear trot awkwardly into the forest, its huge black rump rocking from side to side as it disappeared.

Chapter Seven

A Dance

Maggie didn't see Marc for four days. There was not a moment when she could sneak out of the house without being spotted by someone working nearby. Both Papa and Madame insisted that she stay indoors and rest until she regained her power of speech. By craning her neck at the window, she could just see the corner of the cabin where Marc had been taken, but no matter how many times she looked, she never saw him outdoors. She guessed he, too, was being treated like an invalid.

She worried about what Aunt Kate and Marc's parents must be thinking. Would Uncle Jeff know she was missing? She was very anxious to get home.

Why did things never work out the way she wanted them? This summer was turning out to be a disaster. First, Uncle Jeff and Colleen had forsaken her. Then, somehow, she had gotten stuck here in an old-fashioned cabin with no television, no books, and no clue as to what would happen next. Things will probably get even worse, she thought, pouting.

So far, she had been willing to pretend she was this girl, Marguerite, because that's what Marc wanted. If only she could talk things over with him. She knew that she had to find a way to get together with him. Then they would find a way to get home!

After four days of listening carefully and observing everything happening around her, Maggie began to speak. "*Ca vorse*," she said in a soft, hesitant voice. She was looking at rain beating on the windows. She had heard Papa use the words earlier when he had opened the door and the rain had blown in, drenching him. The family laughed with pleasure when she spoke, and Maggie felt relieved. She must have used the words correctly, more or less.

The rain soon ended and the weather cleared. That afternoon, Madame let Maggie come into the sunshine. She brought the rocking chair from the fireplace and placed it for Maggie in front of the cabin, facing the sparkling bay.

Many men, women and children were hoeing and pulling weeds in the narrow fields that stretched down to the shore. In the field directly in front of the cabin were the four boys. The oldest was Jacques, then Charles, Pierre and Michel. They all wore hats pulled down to their eyebrows like the men. Wet patches of sweat showed on the backs of their shirts and down their sides.

Marc and the man who thought he was Marc's papa were nearby, ploughing between some stumps of trees. An old black horse was hitched to the plough. A pair of oxen were pulling another plough that was breaking the sod farther down the clearing, but this was the only horse Maggie could see from where she was sitting. Its coat was dull and shaggy, and flecked with gray. Its ribs made bony ridges in its sides. Marc was leading the horse, but he was also helping it by heaving on a rope that passed over his shoulder and was attached to the plough. His face was red from the strain. The man was holding the handles of the plough, forcing it into the ground. His muscles bulged against his rough shirt and perspiration ran down his face.

"Hoo-ee! Noiraud. Hoo-ee!" the man shouted, encouraging the emaciated animal to keep going. At the end of each furrow, they let Noiraud have a rest while the man rubbed the animal's face and spoke softly to it.

"Hurry, Charles! Pierre! More water," called Madame from the doorway. The boys dropped their hoes and loped over to their mother. Pierre took a bucket from her hand. Since Jean-Marc and Marguerite had gotten lost, the villagers agreed to a new rule that no child was allowed to go alone into the forest, even if only to fetch water from La Source.

"You're not sick," said Charles to Maggie as he passed her. "You're pretending so we have to do our work and yours, too."

"Yeah, you're just pretending!" Pierre repeated. He gave Maggie a little push on the shoulder and looked up at Charles for approval.

"Boys! The water!" said Madame sternly from the doorway. They ran up the path, the empty bucket swinging awkwardly against Pierre's legs as he tried to keep up with his brother. Their mother smiled as she watched them go.

Madame brought Maggie a skein of wool and asked her to wind it into a ball. Maggie tried for minutes to make the end of the yarn into a ball but only managed a tangled snarl. Madame came to her and, kneeling in the wild grasses beside her, helped her. It seemed so simple once she showed Maggie how to anchor the end of the yarn with her fingers and wrap it around and around. Madame looked closely into Maggie's eyes, frowning. She seemed worried about this daughter who had forgotten how to speak, except for a few simple words, and how to wind a ball of wool, something even Jeanne and Françoise could do.

Maggie wanted to reassure her. She put her hand on the woman's arm and said, with what she hoped was the right tone and accent, "I'm better now."

Madame looked into her eyes a moment. "Yes, I think you are getting well," she said, her frown vanishing. "There's a dance at the home of Jean-Baptiste this evening. Oh, I know what you are thinking. A dance in the busy season, that is unusual. Jean-Baptiste suggested it. He said we must all celebrate the safe return of you and Jean-Marc. I was afraid it was too soon — that you would be too weak to attend. But now" — she nodded her head decisively —"yes, we will go."

The pig appeared from behind a stump. Like the other animals it was let out of its corral each morning to hunt for food. Following a scent it snuffled toward Maggie.

"Shoo," shouted Madame, shaking her apron. The pig ran toward the woods. "Soon it will grow fat on roots and nuts," she said. "How I look forward to fresh pork!" She smiled at the thought. "And lard for baking!"

That evening, after the supper dishes were cleared and the animals were gathered and put into the corral and shed for the night, the family bathed. The fire was kept burning after the meal to heat the water. A wooden tub was put near the fire and half-filled with warm water. A blanket was hung from a rope for privacy.

First Madame bathed the little girls. Then she helped little Michel, who squealed a great deal that she was hurting his ears and getting soap in his eyes. Next came Pierre. Then it was Maggie's turn.

Madame added a little hot water to the tub, put fresh clothing and a rough towel on the rocking chair, and left Maggie alone behind the blanket. Maggie slowly prepared for her bath. She had been longing for days for a bath or a shower, but now she was reluctant. She put one foot in the water, looked down at it and shuddered. A haze of gray soap scum floated on the tepid water. Thinking of the five people waiting their turn, she stepped into the tub. But she couldn't bring herself to sit in the murky water. Scooping it up with her hand, she wet herself, then soaped herself with the strong-smelling yellow soap she found on the floor beside the tub. She rinsed off as best she could, but she was awkward and splashed water on the floor. When she blotted up the spills with her washcloth, she realized just how hard-packed the dirt floor was. It was bone dry where the puddles had been.

"Marguerite! Hurry! The water will be cold." It was Charles, waiting his turn. "Maman! Tell her to hurry!"

"Marguerite? Do you need help?" asked Madame.

"One moment," Maggie answered. She dried and dressed quickly, her skin tingling from the strong soap.

When they were all ready, they left together for the dance. People were streaming from the cabins, all with shining faces and clean clothes. Many told Maggie how happy they were that she was getting better. They walked along the crooked path that joined the cabins until they reached the last cabin in the clearing, a building much larger than the others.

It was packed with people. The walls were lined with benches, and a long table had been pushed aside so that the centre of the floor was clear for dancing. In one corner stood a small platform on which a large bell was resting, as if it was being displayed in a museum.

Maggie spied Marc sitting on a bench. In order to sit beside him, she excused herself and squeezed in beside some old women whose fingers and tongues were flying equally fast as they knit and chatted together. For several moments, Maggie and Marc did not speak of the subject most on their minds. They were afraid of being overheard.

Everyone in the settlement was in the room with them, from tiny babies held in their mothers' arms to old men clustered together and smoking at one end of the room. A muscular man with a bald head and a white beard approached Marc and Maggie and bowed slightly.

"Welcome to our home. We are happy you have recovered and can be with us again." This must be Jean-Baptiste. He welcomed everyone, then he put a fiddle under his chin, and the floor quickly filled with dancers. Some had to wait their turn, for there was not room for all to dance at once. They contented themselves with clapping and stamping their feet on the floor.

Under the screen of noise, Marc and Maggie could whisper unobserved.

"See those people by the door?" Marc asked.

"They look so ragged," said Maggie. The others in the room had, like Marc and Maggie, many mends in their clothes, but these people looked thin and sick.

"Jean-Marc's old grandmother has been talking on and on about the refugees and their escape from the soldiers across the water." He pointed to a frail old lady with wisps of white hair falling from under her cap. "These poor people are the refugees she's been talking about," said Marc. "They live in huts around the point, quite near to here."

"What do you mean? Refugees from what?" she asked.

"I'm not sure. Grand-mère insists that these people escaped in a fishing boat when the British deported the Acadians from Nova Scotia. She says there are others all over Île St. Jean — hundreds, maybe thousands of refugees."

"When the British deported the Acadians from Nova Scotia," Maggie repeated woodenly. "But that was in the seventeen hundreds."

"Yes, 1755 to be exact."

Maggie was stunned. Her mind raced. "You're asking me to believe that these people came here more than two hundred years ago?" she said in an astonished voice. "You've got to be kidding!"

"No, I'm not asking you to believe that. Look, she's an old lady. Oh, she's been treating me great, and she's kind and all that, but I think her mind's going. She's lost track of what century we're living in. She says the refugees came here two years ago. She says that the year, now, is 1757." Marc laughed a little, but he didn't take his eyes off Maggie's face, as if he was watching for her reaction to this ridiculous piece of news.

For a moment Maggie couldn't speak. Of course, he was right — Jean-Marc's grandmother was confused.

They sat silently for a few minutes, watching the dancers. What the old lady had told Marc was unbelievable, and yet it would explain the spartan cabins, the old-style clothes, the different French spoken by these people.

Maggie struggled with her thoughts. She knew how certain Madame was that Maggie was Marguerite, the daughter she had lost. And Jean-Marc's papa truly believed that Marc was his son. She also knew that these people were not old or confused. She sensed that they were sincere and honest. They would not try to trick anyone.

For the first time since they had arrived in the village, Maggie let herself think the unthinkable. As if in a trance, she turned to Marc.

"Marc, I think Jean-Marc's grandmother isn't confused at all."

Marc shook his head and raised his hand as if to protect himself from what she was going to say.

"Marc, I think that somehow we've gone back in time. That we're actually living in 1757." And for the first time since she had come to this strange village, Maggie felt a stab of fear.

Chapter Eight

A Prayer for Protection

"That's impossible," Marc hissed. They both glanced around them to see if anyone was listening, but everyone seemed intent on the dance.

"Don't ask me to explain it, but that must be what's happened." Maggie paused as the tune ended and the dancers moved to the sidelines. Jean-Baptiste mopped his bald head. Someone handed him a cup of tea and made room for him to sit on a bench. After a moment, Jean-Marc's papa bounded to the front of the room with his fiddle and bow. Soon he was playing vigorously. Everyone changed partners and began to dance again.

Maggie looked at Marc closely. "Do you remember any of the Acadian history your mother's been teaching you?"

"Quite a bit. While Grand-mère tells me things — and she hardly ever stops talking — well, I've been remembering more stuff from history books than I thought I knew." He paused for a moment. "But what has that to do with anything? Going back in time is impossible. There must be a logical explanation for what's happening."

"Marc," said Maggie quietly, "impossible things do happen. How else would you explain your legs?"

Marc looked down, then he shut his eyes and his cheeks flushed. He didn't answer.

"Look, Marc," said Maggie, "I don't want to believe it either. I'm scared. But it's the only explanation that makes sense."

They were silent, both struggling with their own thoughts. Marc began staring at the dancers as if mesmerized.

Maggie spoke first. "Just go along with me for a few minutes — about this going back in time thing. From what you've found out, do you think we're still on Prince Edward Island?"

Marc looked doubtful for a moment, then he shrugged. "Okay. I guess it doesn't hurt to talk about it. From the history I remember, and from what Grand-mère says, this is what the situation is — if what you say is true. And that's a big if," he said vehemently, looking directly into her eyes.

Maggie nodded, and Marc went on, speaking more quietly now.

"These people call this place Île St. Jean. That's what P.E.I. was called when it was controlled by France. Later, when the British captured it, they changed its name to Prince Edward Island."

Maggie looked around the room. There were only six cabins in the settlement but there must be forty or fifty people at the dance, counting the refugees. Could they be ghosts? Or, even more frightening, were she and Marc ghosts? She reached over and pinched Marc's arm.

"Ouch!" he shouted. Several people turned and stared at him. "What did you do that for?" he hissed.

"I just wanted to make sure you were real. Tell me more,"

she said, feeling relieved because Marc seemed very much alive. He rubbed the red spot on his arm and looked angry, but in a minute he went on.

"This cabin is larger than the others because it was built as a meeting place for the settlers as well as the home for Jean-Baptiste and his family. Grand-mère says he is rich with children — he has fourteen. He and his family were the first people to settle here. They came from Acadia — that's in Nova Scotia — long before the deportation there. Soon after he arrived, these other families also came from Acadia because the government wanted them to grow food for the soldiers in their big fortress at Louisbourg."

"Louisbourg," said Maggie. "That's a fort in Nova Scotia. I went there, once, on a school trip. There are actors in costumes who play old-time soldiers."

"That's a re-creation of the old fort. If we are actually living in 1757, the original fort is still standing with real soldiers and everything."

When Maggie didn't say anything, Marc went on. "I can tell you something else Grand-mère told me. See that big bell in the corner? The refugees brought that with them. It's from a church the British burned. They risked their lives to go back and get it. They carried it away under cover of darkness, from under the soldiers' noses, they said. They plan to put it in a church of their own someday."

Marc was talking as if he already accepted Maggie's theory that they had gone back in time. The music stopped. Two women passed around cups of a tea made from some herbs one of them brought wrapped in a handkerchief. Each family had brought cups. Other women served cakes made from coarsely ground grain and sweetened with molasses.

Maggie only nibbled her cake. She was too overwhelmed to feel hungry. She remembered Mrs. McKay telling her about the Acadians being deported twice. Although the refugees from Nova Scotia thought they had reached safety on Île St. Jean, she had said, they were deported once again. She had also said that they lived in violent times.

As Maggie slowly sorted out all these strange and disturbing ideas, she realized that these people who were dancing with such gaiety were in grave danger. And if she and Marc stayed here, they'd be in danger, too.

"Marc," she said solemnly, "I watched when they brought us here. I think we could get back to that place in the forest. If we jumped into the whirlpool, I'm almost sure we could get back home."

"I've been thinking about that," he said slowly. "Of course, that's what we'll do. But ...," his voice drifted off. She grabbed for his arm but he jerked it out of her reach. "I'd like to stay. Just for a few weeks."

"I don't want to be here when it happens," she said.

"The deportation? We don't need to worry It's a whole year away. We can stay here for a while."

"You believe me, then?" Maggie asked. "You believe that we are living in the past."

"It's the only explanation that makes sense."

Maggie thought of home, of Uncle Jeff back from Vancouver with his briefcase full of presents, of telling Colleen about her dream. For maybe this was all a dream. That was the explanation! If that were the case, she was ready to wake up!

"Why should we stay here one more day?" she asked Marc sharply.

"You can go on if you want to. I'll stay on my own." He sounded belligerent, more like the Marc she'd been getting to know before all this happened.

She was confused. She desperately wanted to return to the little cottage she had been sharing with Aunt Kate; to escape the coming expulsion of which these happy people were still unaware. Yet when she considered leaving Marc behind, she was troubled. She had got him into this predicament by daring him to go with her. In a way it was her responsibility to make sure he got back home. What would she tell his parents if she returned without him? On the other hand, if the expulsion was a whole year away, she could safely stay a few days, even a few weeks, if Marc insisted. Then they would go home together.

She felt better and began to look around the room with interest. The music began again, and a girl of sixteen or so ran toward them.

"Oh, Marguerite, I am so glad to see you!" She clasped Maggie's hands tightly in her own. "I got home just today from St. Pierre. Tante Emilie's new baby is a girl! She is so sweet, Marguerite! How blue her eyes are! And her smile is the smile of an angel." She paused, laughing a little, still holding Maggie's hands.

Maggie didn't know what to say. This pink-cheeked girl must be Marguerite's friend, but Maggie didn't even know her name. What could she say that wouldn't give away the fact that she was only pretending to be Marguerite?

"Hello," Marc said loudly.

"Oh, Jean-Marc! I am so thoughtless. You and Marguerite have had a terrible experience and here I am chattering away about helping my aunt rather than asking about you. I wanted to see you as soon as I got back this afternoon, Marguerite, but Maman said, 'Not now, Antonine. I need your help.' She said I could wait just a few more hours since she'd get no more work out of me once we got together." Antonine giggled and squeezed Marguerite's hand. "Now we have the time. Tell me everything that has happened since I went away."

"Can your talk wait a few more minutes?" asked Marc politely. "First, you will dance with me?"

"*Bien sûr, monsieur. Merci*," answered Antonine solemnly, dropping him a little curtsy. Then she laughed as Marc swung her into the swirl of dancers. Maggie realized why Marc had been watching the people on the dance floor with such intensity. He had probably never seen anyone dance like this before, but he was doing a good job of following their example.

Maggie was surprised by Marc's thoughtfulness. He was giving her time to collect her thoughts, to prepare for a long talk with a good friend who knew everything about her, but about whom she knew next to nothing. She watched as Marc and Antonine floated around the room, their feet barely touching the floor. Marc's face was filled with joy, and as he passed by, he threw back his head and laughed. Instantly she realized why Marc did not want to go home yet. At home he could not dance.

A young man approached Maggie and asked her to dance, but she shook her head and said she was not yet strong enough. Another asked, then another, but soon they left her alone. After her whirl around the room with Marc, Antonine was asked to dance again and again. When the music finally stopped, she ran toward Maggie, but Madame intervened and said it was time to go home. The girls could talk tomorrow.

When Maggie said goodbye to Marc, she was able to whisper, "We'll offer to go together to get water. Then we'll be able to talk."

As Antonine said goodbye, she murmured in Maggie's ear, "I have something important to tell you tomorrow — something that happened while I was in St. Pierre. It is wonderful!"

Marguerite's family walked home together by moonlight. Papa carried Jeanne, asleep with her head lolling against his neck, and Jacques carried the sleeping Françoise. Madame was singing a ballad, a song of young lovers and death, her voice sweet and sad on the still night air.

Because they were all listening to the story told by the song, they were nearly at their cabin before they heard their cow, Isabelle, bawling loudly.

"Perhaps something has happened to her calf," shouted Papa. He thrust the child he was carrying into Madame's arms and hurried ahead. He scrambled over the fence, ran across the corral and pulled open the shed door. The others clambered over the fence and followed.

Isabelle's calf was running back and forth much agitated by its mother's distress, but it appeared unhurt. Isabelle whirled her head toward the open door, and Maggie saw her eyes flashing white in the dimness. Papa rushed out of the shed. He ran to the gate of the corral. The latch was smashed!

"The pig!" he shouted.

They looked everywhere. The pig was gone! Papa fell to his knees beside a muddy place near the trough. Paw prints were clearly visible in the bright moonlight.

"A bear," he said. "A bear has taken the pig." Then he looked up at Madame. "Take the children in the house quickly." His voice suddenly sounded very tired. "There is nothing we can do until morning."

Before they slept, the family said its evening prayers. That night they added a prayer for mercy and protection from wild animals.

Maggie lay awake in the little cabin long after the others slept. There was an uneasy, hollow feeling in the pit of her stomach. She was thinking of the pig, seemingly so protected by the sturdy corral, but all the while in such terrible danger.

Chapter Nine

The Trap

At breakfast Madame scooped some boiled grain into each person's bowl. Then she passed the jug of milk.

"Where is the molasses?" asked Michel, the child who most resembled Papa with his wiry black hair and blue eyes.

"It is all gone," said Madame. "But see how good the porridge tastes without it."

Michel took a mouthful, squeezed his eyes shut and sucked in his cheeks. Madame gave Papa a stricken look. Papa looked serious for a minute, then he laughed his big booming laugh. With this attention, Michel made another face, and all the children laughed, except for little Françoise, who had a solemn, faraway look on her face.

"Françoise, why are you looking so sad?" asked Papa.

"The pig," said Françoise, her eyes round and serious.

"We won't miss the pig," said Papa heartily.

Madame looked quickly down at her bowl.

"The crops are growing tall in the fields," Papa went on, looking at Madame. "It won't be long till harvest time, then we'll have lots to eat."

After breakfast Maggie sat outdoors in the sun with a basket of mending at her feet. Madame said that she should do light tasks one more day, then she could return to her regular duties.

Maggie pulled a thick woollen sock over her hand and wiggled her fingers through a hole in the heel. She took a smooth round stone that Madame kept in the sewing basket and fitted it inside the heel to make a firm surface for her darning. She made rows of stitches across the hole. Then she began to weave a strand of wool back and forth, over and under the rows of stitches, just as Madame had shown her. Her forehead wrinkled as she struggled to keep the darned area smooth.

She was thinking of Antonine. She was surprised that Antonine, who was at least sixteen years old, had chosen her, a twelve-year-old, for a friend. Probably it was because they were the closest in age of any girls in the settlement. The only other girls Maggie had met were little, like Marguerite's sisters, or were young married women with babies of their own.

Maggie pulled a stitch tight, and the darned area puckered. Frowning, she picked at it with the end of the needle, trying to loosen the strand. She was concentrating so hard that she didn't notice Antonine approaching until she heard a cheerful "Good day!" behind her.

Antonine's rosy face was as vivacious and smiling as at the dance. Unruly light-brown curls spilled out from under her white cap. She sat down on the grass by Maggie's chair and pulled a well-worn shirt from her own sewing basket. Then she began to hunt for scraps the right size to patch the elbows.

"Maman was good enough to spare me for a little while so we can visit," she said to Maggie as she began sewing with tiny, even stitches. "Now tell me about being lost in the woods.

You and Jean-Marc became separated from the others while you were berry picking. Is that right?"

"I can't tell you much. I don't really understand what happened," answered Maggie truthfully.

"Maman says you and Jean-Marc had a terrible shock. Tell me, are you really well now?" Antonine dropped her sewing in her lap and looked up into Maggie's face with grave concern.

"I feel well, but sometimes I am still confused."

"Let's not dwell on things that upset you," said Antonine, going back to her sewing. "Let's pick up where we left off — with the conversation we had just before I left for St. Pierre."

Maggie bent over her darning and was silent as her mind raced. What would the topic of that conversation likely have been? She thought of her long telephone talks with Colleen every night after their homework was done. Clothes? She glanced at Antonine's faded dress, then at the mends in her own. No, they wouldn't have been discussing the latest fads. Nor would it have been their future careers. There weren't even schools here. She decided to make a stab at it.

"Do you mean the discussion about our parents, or the one about boys?"

"Boys, of course," said Antonine, laughing. Then she stopped laughing and suddenly looked very shy. "Dear Marguerite. How I have longed to tell you my news! When I was in St. Pierre, I met someone."

"A boy?"

"A man. Étienne is his name. He is nineteen and he already has some land of his own under cultivation."

"Tell me about him."

"He is very strong. When it is hot and he takes his shirt off to work in the sun, the muscles in his shoulders look like the roots of a giant tree." She stopped, blushing. When she saw that Maggie was not going to tease her about being so immodest as to gaze at a man's bare shoulders, she continued. "He can work longer hours than any man in St. Pierre. And after a full day's work, he can sing and dance all evening! He never seems to tire. And he can be so funny! He always has people laughing around him."

"Where did you meet him? Did you see him often?" asked Maggie, thinking that this Étienne sounded wonderful, indeed.

"He came to Tante Emilie's cabin each evening after we had put the little ones to bed. He would sit beside me." Antonine blushed again. "We would talk with Tante Emilie and Oncle Hubert. They like him, too! They like him so much that, on my last evening there, they left us sitting on the doorstep while they went inside and closed the door so we could talk in privacy. And — oh, Marguerite! — he asked me — oh!" Antonine hid her face in her hands.

"He asked you what?" asked Maggie.

"He asked me to be his wife," said Antonine so softly Maggie could barely hear the words.

Maggie was astounded. She and Colleen sometimes talked about getting married, but that was years away, after university, after she became either an astronaut or a teacher and Colleen became a concert pianist.

"Aren't you awfully young to be thinking of marriage?" she blurted out.

Antonine laughed. "You forget that I am four years older than you. It is time I thought of such things. Papa met him when he came to bring me home. When Étienne asked his permission to marry me, Papa said yes. Of course, he took the advice of Oncle Hubert and Tante Emilie. Papa says I must wait until I am seventeen. But, Marguerite, that is only a few months away! Étienne will be twenty by then. Oh, Marguerite, aren't you happy for me?"

66

Maggie realized that she must be looking rather serious. But, of course, Antonine could not choose a profession other than that of a wife. There was simply no other choice. She could not even choose to go into a convent here in this wilderness. How lucky she was, then, to have found someone she liked and admired so much.

"Of course I am happy for you," Maggie answered, clasping Antonine's hand between her own and smiling.

"Tonine, come here. I need you," called Antonine's mother, Madame Gallant. Antonine folded her mending and stood up. Maggie stood, too. The girls looked at each other for a moment, then hugged, an embrace full of emotion. Unable to speak but smiling tremulously, Antonine turned and ran back to her cabin. Maggie truly liked Antonine, and at this moment she felt as close to her as ... as Marguerite would have felt.

After the noon meal, while the workers were resting before returning to the fields, Marc came with his bucket to ask if Maggie could go with him to La Source.

Madame sent Marc outdoors while she spoke with Maggie. "I'm not sure it's a good idea to spend time with Jean-Marc," said Madame. "Sometimes I worry about you, Marguerite. I have allowed you to work with him because you are friends and he is a fine young man. But I think it is time that you saw less of him. You are twelve years old, old enough to give up running and climbing trees like a boy!"

Maggie was shocked by Madame's words. She resented the idea that running and climbing trees were only for boys. But her annoyance was dwarfed by the fear that she wouldn't have a chance to talk alone with Marc. She realized quickly that there would be no use trying to change Madame's idea of how a young Acadian lady should act, so she tried a different argument.

"I have stayed quietly near the cabin for many days. Perhaps I need some exercise — like a walk in the woods!"

Madame looked into Maggie's eyes while she mused aloud. "You are pale. You have still not recovered completely. Perhaps a walk in the fresh air would do you good."

Finally Madame gave her permission. But she warned Jean-Marc to bring Maggie straight back. Today she was more afraid than usual of wild animals.

They had almost reached the spring when Maggie brought up the subject that had been on her mind since last night. "I think we should go home now, Marc, before more terrible things happen." She couldn't explain it to Marc, but something else was troubling her. She felt herself being drawn to the people around her, to Marguerite's family and to Antonine. She liked being part of a real family. She wanted to go now, before it got more difficult to leave. Marc looked grouchy and didn't say anything.

"Aunt Kate, your parents, they'll be worried about us," she said.

Marc was silent for a few minutes. "Maybe you're right," he said reluctantly. "I am sick of working all the time!" He looked at his hands, where several blisters had broken and bled and were now beginning to heal.

"Okay, let's go," said Maggie, putting down her bucket in a thicket of grass near La Source and striking out on a path along the stream that flowed nearby.

"Just a minute. Let's discuss this some more," Marc called after her.

But she was striding through the woods. "Stay if you want to," she called. "I'm going home!" She was frightened about the dangers of living in the eighteenth century more than she was willing to admit to Marc. "Aren't you hungry?" she called over her shoulder. "Don't you want to go home where you can eat all you want?"

"I could manage a burger and fries," he called back. "A truckload of burgers and fries!"

In a minute Marc caught up to her and they walked together in silence. "It's just that here I can —" He broke off, uncertain, but Maggie knew what he was thinking of as he stretched out his legs into long strides.

As they rounded a bend in the trail, Maggie noticed something, perhaps a dead animal, in a little hollow beside a tree. Flies were buzzing around it. She stepped off the path to get a better look, then gave a little shriek. Marc ran to her. There, half-hidden in the undergrowth was the carcass of the pig, partly eaten, with its pink belly ripped open and its insides gone. Beside it, a paw dipped in blood had left its mark on some leaves just as a finger dipped in ink leaves its mark on paper. They looked around uneasily.

"Let's get out of here," said Maggie, and they began to run along the path in the direction in which they'd been going. When they could run no more, they walked. The trail turned away from the stream, and suddenly they could see the giant pine tree towering above everything. They left the path and scrambled through the trees and bushes to reach it. When they broke through into the little grassy clearing, they ran toward the tree, then stopped, puzzled. There was no hole in the ground, no whirlpool.

"It must be a different pine tree," Marc said. The walls of the forest completely surrounded the little clearing. The leaves of the trees rustled menacingly. They looked around.

"*Bonjour,*" said a voice from behind them. They whirled around to see a Mi'kmaq boy who looked to be about thirteen or fourteen. His black hair hung to his shoulders. He wore leather pants and moccasins, and a shirt like Marc's. He carried a small axe.

"It's good to see you," he said in French. "I heard about your adventure. I'm glad that you seem to be feeling better."

Maggie liked him instantly. Everyone else referred to Jean-Marc and Marguerite being lost in the woods as an ordeal. This boy called it an adventure.

"I was just on my way to your cabins to bring you some medicine from my mother. It'll bring back your memory. Make tea with it and drink it in the morning and again at night until you are completely well." He handed Marc a leather pouch tied with a thong.

"*Merci*," said Marc, tucking the pouch into his belt. The Mi'kmaq boy turned away a minute as if wondering whether to speak again. Then he turned back.

"Why did you come here, so deep in the forest? You're far from your village."

Maggie didn't want to say anything about the whirlpool. Marc must have felt the same way because he told the boy about the bear stealing the pig and of finding its carcass.

"I guess we were afraid. So we ran," he said.

"Show me the pig" was all the boy said. They began to walk back along the stream. When they reached the pig, the boy said, "Don't touch it. There must be no scent of people." He disappeared into the forest and returned a minute later with a wide strip of birchbark and some sticks. He put the bark on the ground beside the carcass. Then with the sticks he rolled the carcass onto it.

They heard the sounds of people coming along the path before they could see them. It was Jacques and Charles, Marguerite's brothers. Jacques, the oldest in the family, was developing the strong shoulders of a man used to hard physical work. He was as tall as Papa. When he was away from his parents, he liked to tell the younger ones what to do. They always obeyed him because, if they didn't, they knew he would tell Papa and they would be in trouble.

"*Bonjour*, Lkimu," Jacques said to the Mi'kmaq boy. Then he turned angrily to Marguerite. "So this is where you are.

Maman became worried when you didn't return from La Source. Charles and I have been calling in the forest and looking for you by the shore — everywhere. The men are getting ready to form another search party. Why don't you think, Marguerite? You're always getting into trouble." Then he saw the pig's carcass and his voice faded.

"We're going to build a trap for the bear," said Lkimu.

Jacques told Maggie to go home, where she belonged. Maggie begged to help build the trap. Marc told Jacques how she had found the pig. He pointed out that they might soon have fresh bear meat for supper. Finally, Jacques agreed to let her stay.

Charles ran back to tell Maman that Marguerite and Jean-Marc were safe, and that Jacques would watch over everyone while Lkimu showed them how to build a bear trap. Meanwhile, Lkimu chose a site for the trap under the large maple tree. Using his axe, he cut some strong young saplings. Soon Charles was back with another axe and two knives.

They worked through the morning, building something that looked like a log box with one side open. Lkimu showed them how to notch the small logs and fit them together so that pushing against a wall of the box would only tighten the joints. They dragged the sheet of birchbark with the pig on it into the trap, then slid it from under the carcass. The pig would be the bait. They then built a gate above the open side of the trap, and they propped it on a pole set diagonally across the opening.

"When Monsieur Bear steps in to finish his dinner," said Jacques, "he will knock the pole aside as if it were a twig!"

"Then the gate will fall," said Charles, "and when the bear tries to get out, he will push the gate tight against these poles and he will be trapped."

"That'll show him!" said Marc.

Lkimu looked at Marc. "If the bear comes into the trap, it will be because he knows we need food and he is willing to give himself to us. It does not mean that we are smarter than he is."

"We'll catch him, for sure. Then you will come, Lkimu, and join us for a feast of bear meat at the home of Jean-Baptiste," said Jacques, laughing with pleasure.

By the time they had finished building the trap, it was early evening. They were all ravenously hungry as they started back to the village. Maggie was walking behind Jacques, Charles and Marc when she remembered Lkimu. She looked back, but he was not there. She felt a sharp pang of disappointment. She remembered his gentle words about the bear, as if he had been talking about another person. She wanted to hear more, but he had disappeared into the forest.

When they got home, Maggie and Marc were both given stern lectures for not coming right back from La Source. But neither was punished for their dangerous behaviour. Finding the pig was considered a great stroke of luck.

They both looked very serious that evening. Their families thought it was because Marguerite and Jean-Marc had finally learned their lesson about straying too far into the forest. Their families could not know what the children knew. That they were in a different kind of trap. They did not know how to get back to the twentieth century without the whirlpool, and they did not know how to find the whirlpool.

Chapter Ten

Maggie and the Bear

Late in the night, when the only sounds in the little cabin were soft snores and the occasional rustle of a straw-filled mattress, Maggie's eyes flew open. She had been dreaming that she was lost in the forest. In the dream she was very hungry and she was searching for food. Then, on the path in front of her, illuminated by a ray of sunlight, she saw a bowl of steaming soup. She fell on her knees beside it, but the minute her fingers touched the bowl, a door shut behind her with a loud clang. She whirled around and saw she was in a prison cell. Through the bars of the cell she could see a guard walking away, twirling a ring of keys around his finger. He stopped, wound up like a baseball pitcher, and threw the keys away. She could see them arc against the sky, then fall far out in an ocean, an ocean as large as the world. She woke, her heart beating with fear and horror at being locked in the cell forever.

The walls of the cabin were dark shadows in the faint light from the dying fire. The room was stuffy and the air seemed to press down on her face, making it difficult to breathe. She eased herself up and crawled over Françoise, who was deep in sleep. She dressed as quickly as she could and crept outside, shutting the door quietly but for a little creak of a hinge.

The moon was bright, and around the dark cabins, nothing stirred. The night air was cool. She sucked it deep into her lungs again and again. She was hungry, as she had been in her dream. But that wasn't what was upsetting her. It was the bear. Perhaps the bear was caught in the trap and was feeling as desperate as she had in the cell of her dream. She had to see for herself.

It was easy to find the way to La Source for the path was well worn, but finding the spot where they'd built the trap was more difficult. It was darker here, deeper in the forest, and the undergrowth seemed to grab and pull at her skirt like hands. All around her were the rustles and swooshes of night-stalkers hunting for food.

When she saw the trap, the first thing she felt was amazement and relief that she had found it. Then she saw that the gate had been released. It was closed. She couldn't see what was inside the cage. It was shaded from the moonlight by the maple tree that towered over it. Something snorted, so near it made her jump. She realized with a shock that the bear was in the trap. One of its eyes glistened as it waved its head, catching her scent. She remembered the bear at the cabin window, its unseeing eye at the pane.

Her mind was a jumble. This bear had stolen the precious pig. It had threatened the safety of the settlement. Its meat could feed the whole village. Yet she was sorry it had been caught. The bear was making snuffling sounds. She could see its dark shape turning this way and that in the small space, waving its head from side to side. It was big and wild and terrifying. But it was wonderful, too. In the Prince Edward Island of her own time, these great dark forests were gone, and all the bears had been hunted and killed years ago.

The bear heaved against the gate but the cage held. She could feel the animal's panic, its desperation. She forgot her hunger. She remembered the feeling of being locked in jail. One day, not only this magnificent animal but all its kind on the Island would be destroyed. She knew she couldn't change all that. But she could help this bear. Just this one.

She crept toward the cage. The bear growled and opened its mouth, its teeth gleaming from the darkness. Lkimu had tied a rope made from braided leather to the top pole of the gate. The end of the rope was looped over a branch. She thought of Uncle Jeff warning her about bears when he took her on a camping trip in northern New Brunswick. "If you meet one on the path, don't play around. They're dangerous animals. Lie still with your stomach and face protected," he had said. "Play dead." She thought of the pig's carcass, its insides ripped out. Her breath was coming in short gasps, but she was determined.

Staying well away from the cage, she climbed the tree, then eased her way around until she was above the cage. Grasping the leather rope, she leaned forward on a stout branch. One arm was on either side of the branch, and her cheek was against its rough bark. She wound the rope around her wrists and pulled. Almost at once she realized that she couldn't move the gate this way. She could hear the bear's body thudding and rasping against the sides of the cage. She sat up and thought. Then she looked up. The next branch on this side of the tree was a long way up, perhaps two metres, but it looked strong and projected directly above the trap.

With the rope in her hand, she climbed the far side of the tree, where the branches were closer together. She threw the rope over the strong branch, then returned to her original position and began pulling, down this time. There was a brief movement in the rope before it stuck again. She reached her arms high above her head, looped the rope around her wrists and let her weight hang from it, all the while keeping her legs firmly around the branch. With a rasping scrape the gate gave way and shot up. The taut rope went suddenly slack, and Maggie flew through the air. She thudded against the ground. The fall jarred through her body and forced the air from her lungs.

She lay still, her chest heaving. At last she drew in a long ragged breath just as the pain exploded in her head. She raised her head in time to see the bear push its head and shoulders under the half-raised gate. The bear heaved, the gate moved up, and the bear scrambled free. She dropped her face to the ground and tried to control her breath. She felt the bear nosing the back of her head. She could smell its rank wild scent. It snorted near her ear. The skin on her neck tightened and she did not breathe, although her eyes were swimming in a sea of red. She sensed it leaving even before she heard it shuffling away.

She lay a long time without looking up. An owl hooted far away. Gradually her breath steadied and her head cleared. She sat up and brushed the twigs from her face and clothes. The pig's carcass looked untouched in the trap. The bear must have been too frightened to eat. She carefully propped the pole under the gate and stepped back to look. No one would ever know the trap had been sprung.

"Goodbye, Monsieur Bear," she said very softly, looking toward the gap in the trees where it had disappeared. "I'm glad you're free." There was no answer. Only the quiet scurrying of the hunters and the hunted in the dark and secret forest.

Chapter Eleven

Part of
a Family

Maggie woke to the *thud*, pause, *thud* of axes on trees. She was alone in the cabin. She stretched and pain slid through her side and up her arm. Then she remembered her middle-of-the-night escapade. She gingerly moved her arm and leg and decided that she was all right, just bruised and stiff. The family must still be pampering her to let her oversleep like this. All the breakfast dishes but her bowl had been cleared away. The porridge in it was cold and had a skin over it, but she gobbled it up, then scraped out the remaining bits with her finger. As she was putting on her clothes, she found a large bruise on her left hip and the side of her head hurt when she touched it. Luckily there were no visible marks to explain to the family. When she thought of what had happened in the night, she felt a twinge of doubt. She realized in the clear light of morning that she didn't want anyone to find out what she had done.

Outdoors, Madame was poking at a fire blazing under a huge steaming kettle which hung from a tripod. Nearby were two wooden tubs and a pile of the family's dirty clothes.

"Good morning, Marguerite. Are you well?"

"Good morning," answered Maggie in the formal, respectful voice she had learned to use with Marguerite's parents. "Yes, I am well. How can I help this morning?"

"Could you do the washing? Antonine's mother and I would like to finish carding and spinning the wool today. There are only a couple of months left before the bad weather comes. We must hurry and get the wool ready for knitting. We still have to wash it before we can use it. That will be another day's work. All the boys need warm socks, and you must have mittens and new stockings."

One day when Maggie had been down to Jean-Baptiste's on an errand, she had seen a few sheep grazing in a field. They must provide the wool for knitting, she thought. Ever since she had come here, Maggie struggled to make connections like this one. She was always straining to make sense of comments and scraps of overheard conversations, then to link them with her observations. She was getting good at making educated guesses and at hiding her ignorance, but the language still gave her difficulty. She sometimes lacked the vocabulary to describe the simplest objects or to express a thought, and sometimes she was reduced to sputtering, "Oh, you know what I mean."

Then people would pat her on the head and say to Madame or Papa, "She has had a shock. It takes a long time to recover fully. But look how well she is doing!" It seemed easier for Marc. He also had some problem with words, but while Maggie had to concentrate hard to get the archaic accent just right, it seemed to roll off his tongue with no effort.

Now she was supposed to wash the clothes and she had no idea how to go about it. She pondered for a moment, then she had an inspiration.

"If you are working with Antonine's mother," she said politely, "perhaps Antonine can work with me?"

Moments later Antonine approached with an armload of laundry. Maggie let her take the lead in the washing procedure. When she saw what to do, she followed along. They filled one of the wooden tubs with hot water from the giant black kettle. Then they poured what was left of the hot water plus some cold water into the rinse tub. Next they put a couple of buckets of water from La Source into the now empty kettle and built up the fire under it. While the water was heating, they sorted the white clothes from the others, and they each dipped a white article in the washtub of hot water. Then they spread the articles on a large flat rock and rubbed them with soap.

It was the same strong lye soap used for bathing, washing hair and all household cleaning. Maggie had watched the women making it from sheep fat and water that had seeped through a barrel of ashes. The first time she had seen it freshly made in large baking pans and cut into neat, creamy-yellow squares, she thought it looked good enough to eat. Now that she knew how it stung her hands and how the fumes made her nose wrinkle, she had no desire to eat it!

The clothes were very dirty. People here wore the same clothes day after day in the dusty fields, changing only when they had their weekly baths. By the end of the week even the towels were red brown from Island soil hastily wiped from hands and faces. Maggie watched Antonine rub extra soap into the dirtiest stains, then bunch the cloth and scrub the spot against the rock until the stain faded. After scrubbing, the clothes were thrown back into the washtub, and the girls stirred and pummelled them in the hot water with two sturdy sticks.

"Did you hear about your bear trap?" asked Antonine.

"No." Maggie stopped stirring.

"When the boys checked it this morning, it was empty. Not even the carcass of the pig was there."

"How could that happen?" Maggie fished an apron from the tub and let it dangle from her stick while she examined it, turning her face away from Antonine while she did so.

"An animal must have dragged it away. An animal so small and wily that it didn't even touch the pole that held the gate. One thing we know for sure: the bear was never in that trap! It's so disappointing! I don't think we'll ever catch it now."

Maggie said nothing and went back to work. After a while, when she thought her arms would surely break, Antonine said that was enough. Now they had to wring the water from the clothes by twisting them. The water was almost unbearably hot, and Maggie shrieked and dropped things in the tub and had to start over. Antonine laughed and teased her and called her a fine lady with soft hands.

After wringing, they dropped the white clothes, the women's caps and the few other precious items made of linen, into the pot of boiling water and left them to simmer. Boiled clothes! thought Maggie with astonishment. Like a pot of pea soup!

"There now," said Antonine with satisfaction, "that will make them white as new!"

Most of the clothes were made of coarse wool. Now Maggie knew why Madame wanted to wash her wool before using it. That would shrink it before the garments were made so they could later be safely washed without them shrinking out of shape. After wringing the woollen items, the girls dropped them in the rinse tub, stirred them around, then they had to wring them again. By the time the clothes had been washed, boiled, rinsed and spread on the corral fence to dry, it was time for the noon meal.

Maggie was aching with fatigue. Her skirt and apron were soaked and her hands were red and stinging. But, tired as she was, she hadn't finished her day's work.

All afternoon, she helped Madame. Using some fragments of worn-out linen for a pattern, they cut pieces out of some heavy woollen cloth. After supper, they began the laborious task of sewing the pieces together with hundreds of tiny stitches. They were making a new winter jacket for Madame.

That night, Maggie lay in bed too tired to move. As she was drifting off, she heard Madame say, "Marguerite. There are some holes in our blankets. Tomorrow, if the sun shines, we must wash and mend them."

Maggie didn't answer. She couldn't muster the energy to say a word. She could hear the even breathing of the little girls and Papa's snores. It had been an exhausting day. But when she thought of the clean clothes, sweet-smelling from the sun, and of Madame's new, warm jacket, she felt good. They all worked hard, the people in this family. And she was becoming part of it. She fell asleep smiling.

Chapter Twelve

An Afternoon Off

Marc loped along the beach, his eyes searching a stride ahead for flat rocks for his bare feet to land on. He had become so good at this that his stride was smooth and unbroken. He could feel the strength in his sturdy legs. He had been running a long time, first down the beach, then back up, and he was breathing heavily, but he kept on running. Nothing gave him more joy. Finally he stopped and sprawled across a large rock.

He could feel his heart pounding but he couldn't hear his gasping breath over the sighing and swishing of the bay. The wind was up today. That meant the surf was up out on the Gulf of St. Lawrence, and the bay, which was sometimes silent, flat and breathless, was now restless. Swells tumbled over themselves onto the shore and slid to within a few inches of where he lay. He squeezed his eyes shut against the sun, luxuriating in the warmth and freedom of the moment.

He was not supposed to be here. He had no right to be resting. During all the hours of daylight he was supposed to be working. That was a bit of an exaggeration, he realized, even as he thought it. By the time his Acadian papa woke him in the morning, the sun had been up for some time. But each day when he woke he felt it must be dawn, for his body still ached from the work of the day before; his eyes were gritty and his muscles stiff.

Every day there was hoeing to be done. At first this job seemed easy, but when the work stretched from one hour to two to three, all in the blazing sun, his back grew sore, his hands blistered and his head ached.

When he was not hoeing, there was wood to be split and stacked beside the cabin. The axe handle chafed his blistered hands until they bled. Then old Grand-mère bathed his hands and bound them with strips torn from one of her old petticoats, muttering to herself, bewildered at how his hands could have become so soft in the short time that he had been lost in the forest.

Bandaged hands were no excuse for not working. Work was constant in the settlement. To make more farmland, the forest must be pushed back, and trees had to be felled. The men carried the small trees to a pile where they would later be cut into logs. When the felled trees were large, a team of oxen would haul them out of the way. Dozens of stumps were left dotting the clearing.

One of Marc's duties was to chop branches from the main trunks. He hated every minute of it. The only job he liked doing was taking care of Noiraud. Like him, the old horse always seemed stiff and tired, but unlike him, it was always willing. He admired the animal's dumb stoicism.

Marc resented his Acadian papa for making the poor old animal work such long hours, just as he blamed Papa for making him work so hard. Each evening Marc fed and watered Noiraud and rubbed him down with a handful of hay. While he worked, he talked quietly to the horse and told him his troubles. This noon, after an inadequate meal, Papa told him that their pea plants were in danger of being choked out by a fast-growing weed. Marc must once again spend the day hoeing weeds. He felt a great rush of resentment.

"*Mon papa* ..." he began, then his voice trailed away. He had almost said, "My dad doesn't make me work all the time. He lets me have time to do things I like to do."

"Yes?" said his Acadian papa, thinking Marc was addressing him.

"Nothing," said Marc, relieved that he had caught himself before he'd given himself away. He tramped out to the field, angrily jabbing the end of the hoe handle into the ground with each stride.

An hour later the men who had been working nearby left Marc alone in the fields while they went to help a neighbour fell a particularly huge oak tree. The wood of an oak was so hard that the settlers dreaded having to fell one. The job could take hours. The women weren't in the fields this afternoon. They were salting beef for the long winter ahead. This activity was done in secret. Marc knew he must not speak of it to anyone. The authorities at Louisbourg had forbidden the settlers to kill their cattle. They wanted the herds to grow so Louisbourg would have more beef in the future. But the people needed food. And the butchered animal would provide them with more than that: it would give them tallow for candles and leather for footwear.

Marc looked around. For the first time since he had come here, he was alone. If he moved quickly, he could get away without anyone noticing. Here was his chance for a few hours of freedom!

He scurried down the slope, hid his hoe in a bush, then climbed down the side of the cliff to the rocky shore of the bay. There were two canoes and a small sailing boat on the shore. These craft belonged to all the settlers, and they were used for transportation. As Papa said, "Water makes a smoother road than tree stumps."

Marc pushed one of the canoes away from the shore and clambered into it. He skirted the red cliffs, looking often over his shoulder but no one was watching. Now, here he was, resting on a beach that was safely hidden from the settlement by a jut of land. No one would notice he was missing until it was time for the evening meal, and he would be back before that.

The warmth of the sun helped him relax. He was drifting, floating into sleep. Then he felt something nudge his ribs. His eyes flew open and he saw a foot beside his head. His eyes climbed upward. It was Gérard Pitre, a boy from the village who was a year or two older than Marc. He was smiling and swinging a skin pouch closer and closer to Marc's face.

Marc jumped to his feet, laughing with relief. "I saw you leave," said Gérard. "I waited for my chance, then got my sack of beechnuts. Joseph and I followed you in the other canoe." Marc saw Joseph, Gérard's eleven-year-old brother. "I've got enough beechnuts here," said Gérard, still swinging the pouch, "for the three of us to play."

"What's going on?" It was Lkimu calling. He was beaching his canoe.

No one answered for a moment. Marc could see that Gérard and Joseph were nervous. They shuffled their feet in the sand as the Mi'kmaq boy approached. Marc caught their concern. Would Lkimu tell the adults that the boys were playing when they should be working? Marc didn't know Lkimu well enough to guess.

"What are you doing?" Lkimu asked again. He looked very serious. When they didn't answer, he turned to Marc. "I saw you from the water. At first I thought you must be sick to be lying on the beach in the afternoon."

"No, not sick," said Marc. "But I will be if I don't have some time off!"

Lkimu stared at Marc for a moment. "Time off?" he asked, puzzled.

"We're always being told what to do," said Marc. "Sometimes we should be able to do what we want."

Lkimu laughed then, as if this idea of time off was funny. His laugh was infectious, and the other boys cautiously joined in. Lkimu stopped laughing and looked toward his canoe as if considering whether he should leave. Then he turned back to the boys.

"Can four play this game?" he asked.

The boys found a place where there were few rocks and quickly cleared a space in the sand. Then they scooped out four holes and paced off four throwing points. They each took fifteen nuts. Then each boy in turn stood at his own throwing point and tried to toss as many nuts as possible into his hollow. At the end of each play, the boy with the most beechnuts within his hollow was allowed to confiscate those of his adversaries. This continued until one boy had all the beechnuts. Then the game began again.

Sometimes the boys argued when a nut lay on the rim. Sometimes they scuffled over nuts that landed far from the mark, but they always wound up laughing and shooting again. Joseph was the best thrower. After winning several times in a row, he began to taunt the other boys.

"You're all hopeless. You couldn't win even if your arms were as long as the road to Port La Joye!"

On Joseph's next turn, Lkimu "accidentally" bumped into

his arm so Joseph's beechnut landed well to the side of his goal. Lkimu streaked forward and did a comical dance and made faces to distract the boys' attention. Then he nudged the wayward beechnut with his foot until it rolled into Marc's hollow. The boys whooped with laughter.

After an hour or so of the game, the boys stripped off their clothes and ran into the water. They ducked each other; they yelled and shouted, and they tried to swim, but today, with the surf up, the water was better for jumping in than swimming. When they began to tire, they went ashore and pulled their clothes on over their wet cool bodies.

Gérard looked at the sun. "I think we should go back now, before they notice we're gone," he said. There was a note of tension in his voice.

Joseph scurried about, gathering up the nuts and putting them back in the sack.

"I must go, too," said Lkimu. Marc walked with him to his canoe. "I must go into the forest, to the river where my family has traps."

"What are you trapping?" asked Marc.

"Beaver, otter, mink. Small animals give us their skins to trade for the things we need."

"What kind of things?" asked Marc.

"Cloth for clothes." Lkimu rubbed his hand on his gray woollen shirt. "Dried peas and flour to fill our hungry bellies."

Marc couldn't hide his surprise. "But I thought your people hunted for your food."

"They did in the old days. We still hunt and fish, but not as much, now. Our days are filled with trapping and preparing skins for the traders." Lkimu looked at Marc with a puzzled expression. "Why are you asking so many questions? Have you forgotten these things, Jean-Marc?"

Marc turned his face away so Lkimu couldn't see his eyes. "I still have trouble remembering things — since I was lost in the forest."

"The forest is where things happen that we don't understand," said Lkimu. "I have seen strange things deep in the forest. Sometimes they frighten me ..." His voice trailed off.

Before Marc could ask more questions, Lkimu pushed his canoe from shore and waved once before he disappeared behind the point.

The other boys set out for home in their canoes, staying as close as possible to the shoreline to avoid the worst of the waves. They left the canoes pulled up into the hollow of the cliff exactly where they had found them. Then they scrambled up the cliff, finding footing on points of rocks protruding from the bank. Marc was up first and turned to offer a hand to his friends. As they came over the edge of the bank, he saw their eyes widen with fear. Marc swung around. Monsieur Pitre, Gérard and Joseph's father, was waiting for them with a willow switch in his hand and behind him, walking toward them, was Marc's Acadian papa. Both men looked stern.

"Are these the sons I have raised?" shouted Monsieur Pitre, whacking his switch against the ground. "Running off in the middle of the day without permission? Idling away their time when there is work to be done?"

Although he was speaking to his sons, it was Marc who answered. His Acadian papa was standing silently, but he was also carrying a willow switch, and Marc was angry. Never before had he taken time to be with his friends until the day's back-breaking work was over, supper had been eaten, and Noiraud had been fed and rubbed down for the night. After that, there was little time or energy left for play.

"We were just having a bit of fun," he said.

"Fun!" shouted Monsieur Pitre, still looking at his own boys. "When your bellies are empty in the long winter nights, you will not call this fun. Now, I will help impress this day on your minds so you will not make such a mistake again. Into the shed with you!"

Gérard and Joseph marched toward their shed, their eyes downcast, their papa following with the switch over his shoulder. Marc's Acadian papa finally spoke. He sounded discouraged. "It is necessary, my son. We also must go to our shed."

Inside the shed Papa pulled the door closed. There were no windows in the building but it was roughly built and in the gloom strips of light glimmered between the logs. The shed was empty at this time of day; Noiraud and the cow were tethered outside, grazing on the summer grass.

Marc was frightened. Since his real parents didn't believe in spanking, he had never in his life been punished physically. Papa was scowling, but he looked more puzzled and confused than angry.

"My son, why have you changed?" he asked. "I don't understand it. You have always been obedient." He sighed. "When you were still a baby and your mother died, I wanted to die too." He turned away from Marc and leaned the switch upright against the log wall. He stood there staring at it while he spoke.

"But I had you to live for and I dreamed of you growing to manhood by my side, strong and good and a proud Acadian." He turned back to Marc. "When your stepmother died, along with the little girl she had just given birth to, well, I consoled myself with the knowledge that I will meet them in heaven. Life is hard. Le Bon Dieu tests our courage. But He has also been kind. He has left me you, my son, and my dear mother is still with us. I have much to be thankful for." He sighed again, and began to pace back and forth.

"Now, you have changed. You have become angry and resentful and lazy. You run off to play when it is your duty to work. It is as if you have become younger, more childish than you were before you were lost in the woods."

He stopped pacing and gently grasped Marc by the arms. "Tell me why. What has happened to you to make you this way?"

Marc did not know what to say. He had heard Grand-mère speak many times of his mother in heaven, but this was the first time he had heard about Papa's second wife and baby. He could feel the man's sadness like a presence alongside them in the barn.

Suddenly everything came clear. Papa had not asked him to do any more than any other boy his age in the settlement. Everyone here had to work hard just to survive. Papa himself worked all day long, and did much heavier work than Marc. And he never complained. Even Grand-mère, who was very old and no longer strong, worked long hours to feed and clothe them and to keep their cabin neat and clean. Marc suddenly felt bitterly ashamed.

"I'm sorry," he said, his voice hardly louder than a whisper. "I don't know how to explain the way I've been acting, but from this day on, I will try to make you proud of me. I promise."

Papa looked deeply into his eyes, then a little smile flickered across his face. "I believe you, my son. Now, what will we do about your punishment?" He picked up the switch.

"I am ready," said Marc, wondering if he could take his beating without crying out.

"I think you have learned your lesson without it," said Papa. "But I don't want your friends to be angry with you because they were punished and not you. We must give something to console them."

Papa picked up the switch and brought it down smartly against the partition between the two stalls in the shed. *Whack.* Again and again. *Whack, whack.* "Take that," he shouted at the wall. "Let this be a lesson to you." *Whack.*

Papa and Marc walked together from the shed back into the sunlight. Gérard and Joseph were hoeing nearby. They looked at Marc with sympathy. Marc carefully arranged his face in an expression of regret. He had to concentrate very hard to keep from smiling.

But when he was away from the boys, on his own, his urge to smile dissipated. He realized now that if he stayed here, he had to live up to his responsibilities. This feeling was new. Back at home, ever since his accident, people had done things for him; they had tried to make him happy. No one had suggested that he should accept responsibility for what he made of his life. But here much was expected of him. He suddenly wanted desperately to live up to those expectations. If he could do that, he sensed that he would come to feel better about himself and about everything else.

His promise that he would try to make Papa proud of him was genuine. What frightened him was the thought that he might not be strong enough to keep it.

Chapter Thirteen

Tante Josephine

They had just finished the evening meal. Jeanne and Françoise were washing the dishes and Maggie was sweeping the floor with the raspy-sounding twig broom when Michel burst through the door. His hair was sticking up in clumps, as it always did when he was excited.

"Guess who just arrived? In a canoe. She's coming now."

Madame looked up from her spinning wheel, then at Papa, who was mending a frayed rope. A little smile flickered across her face.

"Let me guess. Is it Tante Josephine?"

Michel's face fell. He had been hoping to surprise everyone. The other boys laughed. The little girls ran to the window and Maggie followed. There, making slow painstaking progress toward them was a gaunt middle-aged woman. Her upper body leaned to one side, so that one shoulder was a few inches higher than the other. Guiding her along the path, his hand on her elbow, was a young man, about Jacques' age, sixteen or seventeen. In his other hand was a large bundle wrapped in a blanket and tied with a rope.

They could hear the woman's voice long before she reached the cabin. She was rattling on like a machine gun, thought Maggie (then she realized that there were no such things as machine guns yet). The young man would open his mouth now and then, but the woman would think of something else to say and he would close his mouth without speaking. Like a fish, Maggie thought.

"Tante Josephine hasn't yet lost the power of speech," said Papa. Madame looked sharply at him and he curbed his smile.

When the visitors arrived at the cabin, there was a great flurry of greetings and shaking of hands. Maggie scooped two bowls of soup from the pot over the fire while Madame cut some bread for the hungry visitors.

"What brings you here, Tante?" asked Papa.

"This is such a pleasant surprise," Madame added hastily, as if she was embarrassed by Papa's abrupt question. But Tante Josephine was not in the least insulted.

"I heard that Marguerite and Jean-Marc had been mauled by bears. That they were near death. And that you, Marie," she said to Madame, "that you were spending all the hours of the day nursing them. So, I thought to myself, I thought, Josephine, you may no longer be young but you've got some life in you yet. Get right over there and help Marie with those poor stricken children. So, I packed enough things for a month or two, and Robert here brought me in his canoe. We left Tracadie early this morning, while it was still cold. My, it is cold at night for this time of the year! Robert is such a fine young man. Do you remember? I am the one who brought him into this world. And what a difficult birth it was! His mother would not have survived without me — and neither would the baby. But now, as you can see, he is a baby no longer. Yes, the nights are cold. It must be the phase of the moon. So unusual. But what is this we have here? Marguerite, mauled by bears, up and around and looking no worse for wear? When Robert was born, he came out the wrong way. I am an expert at such things. I saved his life, you know. When we were in the canoe, I kept saying, 'Make sure you are headed in the right direction, Robert. You were born going the wrong way, and I don't trust you yet.'"

Robert blushed to the roots of his hair and tried to hide his face by bending over the bowl of soup Maggie had set in front of him. The family laughed heartily.

"I see you are here and not in the middle of the ocean headed for France," said Papa. "I think Robert has regained his sense of direction!" They laughed again, even Robert this time.

After explaining to Tante Josephine that the rumours she had heard were greatly exaggerated, Madame urged her to stay for a visit now that she had so kindly come all this way to help them out. Tante Josephine accepted readily.

"I will sleep with Marguerite," she said, as if that was settled.

Françoise and Jeanne looked upset, and Madame quickly said, "We will make a pallet on the floor for you, girls. You can pretend you are camping out under the stars." The children cheered up immediately.

After eating, Robert yawned. They had been travelling since dawn, he said, and he was exhausted. Tante Josephine didn't seem tired at all as she chattered on to Madame, telling her the news of all the other families who lived along the north shore of Île St. Jean. Papa urged Robert to go up to the loft and turn in early. But the young man insisted on helping the boys bring the cow and calf into the shed for the night.

After evening prayers, everyone went to bed. But not before Tante Josephine had examined the family's clothes and declared that she would let down the hems in the dresses of all three girls because they were growing so fast they looked like scarecrows. The little girls looked down at their skirts in bewilderment when they heard this and Madame looked embarrassed. Maggie felt the first sharp pang of annoyance.

Maggie had just drifted off into sleep when a bony elbow jabbed her in the side. Tante Josephine was thrashing around, trying to get comfortable. Soon she settled down and Maggie was letting herself slide into her dream world when Tante Josephine began to snore. Maggie could see her in a shaft of moonlight. Her mouth was open and a loud rattling noise came from her throat, followed by a long sigh. Sometimes the sigh turned into a whistling sound. Maggie turned away and pulled the blanket up over her ear, but the rattles and sighs and whistles seemed to echo in the sleeping cabin. Maggie finally slept fitfully. When she woke in the morning, she was still tired. She wondered how long Tante Josephine would be staying.

The next morning, after she had eaten, Tante Josephine left for a round of visits to all the women in the settlement. She had to find out the news and check all the children she had brought into the world to see if they were thriving.

"Perhaps she will leave soon so we can get some sleep," said Papa, when she had left the cabin.

Madame looked angry. "Shame on you, Louis. That woman is the soul of generosity. She has sacrificed her life for the good of others, and you complain about a little snoring!"

"Sacrifice? You call it sacrifice when she likes nothing better than to snoop into every cabin on Île St. Jean. And to tell everyone how to live their lives. I tell you, the sacrifice is on the part of anyone that woman helps."

"She can't help that she has a crooked back and that no man asked her to marry. She has no relatives to support her. She

95

has no home of her own, Louis. That is the reason she must go from cabin to cabin. Have some compassion!"

"It is not her back that scares off the men," said Papa. "It is another part of her anatomy — her tongue." Then he quickly left the cabin before Madame had a chance to say more on the subject.

Later, when Maggie and Antonine were working side by side weeding vegetables, Maggie asked about Tante Josephine. Antonine accepted Maggie's lapses in memory and was happy to fill in the details.

"She was born with a curved spine because her mother forgot to set willow branches over the door to keep out the evil spirits."

Maggie was shocked. "Do you believe that?" she asked. "About the evil spirits I mean."

Antonine crossed herself hastily. "Marguerite! Do not tempt the spirits."

Maggie changed the subject. "Do you like having her visit?"

"Well, she is a help in times of sickness. That's why everyone calls her Tante — out of respect. She came when my little brother died. She was the one who prepared him for burial. Maman was too ill at the time. She does talk too much, that's for sure. But Maman thinks she got in the habit of talking to hide her shame. The shame of not being married."

Maggie worked for awhile. She was beginning to feel sorry for Tante Josephine. If the only career open to men was farming and the only career open to women was being a wife and mother, how sad the lives of those who could not farm or were not chosen to be a wife. Then she had an idea.

"Antonine. How long has Jean-Marc's father been a widower?"

"I'm not sure. For a few years. Why?"

"He must be lonely. Does he know Tante Josephine?"

Antonine stopped hoeing and stared at Maggie. "I don't think he knows her very well. She has never helped at his house that I know of. When his second wife died, Maman helped because Tante was sick with the fever." She continued to stare at Maggie as their minds raced with the excitement of making a match.

They told no one of their plans. They were afraid that someone might tell Jean-Marc's papa, and he would sidestep their plot.

First they went to Jean-Baptiste and asked if there couldn't be a another get-together. He was somewhat surprised at the request, but he finally agreed to invite everyone for an evening of fiddling and story-telling. "It is what the refugees need — something to take their minds off their hardships. But you young ladies might have another purpose. Can it be that you wish to dance with someone special?" He laughed in a merry way, but the girls just smiled mysteriously and went on their way.

Next they asked Jean-Marc's papa if he would please bring his fiddle to Jean-Baptiste's because no one could play the sad old songs so well. He also looked surprised at the request, but he agreed.

Three days later, on the evening of the party, everyone bathed and put on clean clothes. Tante Josephine came out from behind the blanket dressed in her best clothes. Maggie's heart sank. Her skirt, with stripes in dull shades of blue, looked exactly like the one Tante had worn each day since she came. Her blouse even had the same worn spots on each elbow. Maggie had been hoping that she would wear a brighter coloured skirt, like the one Madame was weaving, with red stripes along with narrow blue ones. She wanted Jean-Marc's papa to find Tante attractive.

Since Tante could not dance, she sat with the old ladies and gossiped and chattered. And since Jean-Marc's papa was busy with his tunes, he paid no attention to her. It wasn't until the tea was being served that the girls saw their chance. They invited Marc and Jean-Marc's papa to have lunch with them. Then Maggie invited Tante Josephine to join them. Maggie and Antonine told Marc that every time Tante Josephine threatened to dominate the conversation, one of them would interrupt her. Marc asked why, and when they wouldn't tell him, he refused to cooperate. Maggie and Antonine looked at each other and sighed.

Papa bowed when he was introduced. "How kind of you to visit us," he said shyly, his eyes downcast.

"Oh, it is not a kindness," said Tante. "It is a pleasure to see so many of my old friends. And such a pleasure to find I am not needed to nurse your son and my dear Marguerite. I was led to believe that both were at death's door, you know. And speaking of death, did you know Achile Bernard has passed away? He took a bath in March during a cold spell and did not stay indoors afterwards. Well, he took the croup and coughed until he died. So foolish! If people would only learn that it is safe to bathe only in warm weather and then only infrequently! But then people don't always do what is best for them."

Maggie broke in by asking Papa, "Did you know Monsieur Bernard?"

"No," he answered.

But before he could go on, Tante continued. "There are other ways of preserving health. Now, if everyone wore a little bag filled with salt around their neck, there would be no more fevers, and if all the children would only learn to —"

"What are your interests, Tante, besides nursing?" asked Maggie.

Tante stopped speaking in confusion. "My interests?" she asked.

"Do you like to cook?" asked Maggie. Antonine could see what her friend was doing, and she joined in.

"Do you like doing housework, Tante? And spinning and weaving. Drying food for winter?"

"Well, well," said Tante, "I can cook as well as any woman. Broth is my specialty. I can cook broth that will both cure the fever and mend broken bones. It is the most nourishing —"

"What a fine housekeeper you must be!" said Maggie. "If only every home was lucky enough to have a nurse such as you, why, there —"

"Are the crops growing well in Tracadie?" Papa asked Tante hurriedly, as if he was the one now trying to steer the conversation. The girls immediately subsided.

"Yes. And here?"

"Tolerably well. Let us pray that nothing attacks them this year. Last year they were doing well until the blight set in and we got only half the grain we had expected."

"Ah, the blight!" said Tante Josephine, as if finally they were getting to something of interest. "I have remedies for keeping the blight away from crops. Now, if only the farmers would listen, I could have saved the crops last year. All it takes is the skin of an animal killed in the last phase of the moon. This skin must be buried for three days and three nights. Then it must be dug up and hung from the branch of an oak tree. That branch must then be cut away from the tree — to break the cycle you see. The skin must then be sprinkled for three days, morning and night, with milk taken from a cow suckling her first-born calf —"

"That sounds very interesting," said Antonine in a doubtful voice. "Do you like fiddle music?" she asked quickly, desperately trying to bring the conversation back to Papa.

"You haven't let me finish, Antonine," said Tante, more than a little annoyed. "You young people are forgetting your manners. I was going to say that the branch of the oak tree must then be planted in the middle of the field. Then that field will be spared the effects of the blight. But that reminds me of my theories of raising children. Children should not feel free to speak when their elders are speaking. Why, when I was a child —"

"You'll excuse me, please," said Papa, breaking in when Tante paused to take a breath. "I think Jean-Baptiste wants me to return to my music." He rose and bowed to Tante Josephine and practically ran across the room, leaving Tante Josephine lecturing Maggie, Antonine and poor Marc, who still didn't understand what was going on.

The next morning Robert's younger brother arrived to say he was needed at home. As Robert prepared for the journey, Madame said that when Tante was ready to return home, Jacques would escort her. Everyone, except Maggie and Antonine, seemed very sorry to see Robert leave without Tante Josephine. But, of course, no one said so.

That evening Marguerite and Antonine called on Jean-Marc's family after supper. They didn't yet know the next step in their matchmaking plans, but they thought a visit might give them inspiration. They were met at the door by Grand-mère. One sleeve was rolled to her elbow and a white bandage wound around her arm. She said that Jean-Marc and his papa were down at the beach mending a leak in one of the canoes. When the girls showed no sign of leaving, she politely asked them in for a cup of tea.

When they were seated on three-legged wooden stools, which were the closest thing to chairs in the cabin, Antonine asked the old lady how she had hurt her arm.

"Ah," said Grand-mère, "I am a clumsy old woman! Yesterday as I was putting a kettle of stew on the hearth to simmer, a burning log split in two and part of it fell against my sleeve. It burned through the cloth into my arm."

Maggie winced, imagining the pain. The girls said how sorry they were, and Antonine quietly promised to pray for Grand-mère's quick recovery. The old lady thanked them, then laughed. "It was my own carelessness. I think Le Bon Dieu means to spare me for a few years yet, for I still have much to learn."

Outside the door Maggie turned excitedly to Antonine, but she could see by her friend's dancing eyes that they were both thinking the same thing. Their feet flew over the path as they raced to tell Tante Josephine about Grand-mère's injured arm.

Within minutes Tante Josephine and the girls were back at Grand-mère's cabin and Tante was unwinding the bandage.

"Please! There is no need!" protested the old lady. But Tante was already gently removing the poultice of wet herbs held in place by the bandage, revealing a raw red area.

"Oh, I know you are overwhelmed by my kindness," said Tante, effectively silencing Grand-mère, who couldn't think what to say to that. "But your method of treating a burn is old-fashioned. I have a new method that is much more effective. Your skin will heal and be smooth as a baby's in less than a fortnight if you let me treat you." As she spoke, Tante dabbed an evil-smelling concoction on the burn, then expertly rewound the bandage.

From that day on Tante visited Grand-mère three times a day to minister to her injury. Sometimes Maggie tagged along to help. At first she was worried that Tante would waste her visits by going when Jean-Marc's papa was out. But she needn't have worried. Perhaps Tante Josephine surreptitiously watched his movements and knew when he was home; perhaps she had a sixth sense about such things. Whatever her method, they visited Grand-mère only when Papa was working in or around the cabin.

Maggie and Antonine were elated with the progress of their plan. They felt that it couldn't fail now that Tante Josephine showed signs that she was entertaining the idea of being Jean-Marc's new stepmother. They were sure that it would be only a matter of time before Jean-Marc's papa realized that she was what he needed to be a happy man.

Chapter Fourteen

Tante's Decision

After a few days Grand-mère pleaded that she really didn't need any more treatment since the burned area was healing nicely.

"All the more reason!" said Tante Josephine. "I have seen it happen many times. When patients quit using my salve with the secret ingredients, the burn can come back."

"Come back?" asked the old lady, incredulously.

"Ah yes. Just as bad, if not worse than before. You have seen it, Monsieur?" she said to Jean-Marc's papa.

"No," said the man. "But then, I am not an expert in such things." He was twisting and plaiting some strong-looking reeds into a rope.

Tante Josephine looked around as she continued to bandage the old lady's arm. "You may not know medicine, but I see you are a fine farmer. You have built a sturdy cabin here, Monsieur. I see you provide for your family as best you can in these difficult times. You have a fine family. It reminds me of Jean-Claude, who lost two of his children to diphtheria back in old Acadia. Then his wife took ill and died leaving him with seven to raise on his own. After he brought his brood over here to Île St. Jean he met Madame Roget, a widow woman, and she consented to marry him. Well, she whipped that household into shape in no time. Everyone says how fortunate for Jean-Claude. There is no way he could have handled all the work without her. And, with respect, Monsieur, I find myself wondering how you are managing so well with only your poor old mother to help."

Grand-mère looked stunned for a moment, then her pleasant face changed into one of barely suppressed fury.

Tante went on, "Oh, I am sure you do your very best, Madame, but you are at an age when you shouldn't be doing the heavy work that we younger women find so invigorating. At your stage in life, knitting by the fire and spinning by the doorway should be the limit of your exertions."

Maggie was afraid that Tante Josephine would continue with her prattle until either Grand-mère or Jean-Marc's papa got up and threw her out the door. So she quickly said that she thought she heard her mother calling them, even though she had heard no such thing.

"Ah, my dear Marie needs me!" said Tante. "I can never refuse the call of someone who needs my special talents." And to everyone's great relief, she gathered up her things and left.

That night, Marc stopped at the cabin and asked if Maggie could go with him to La Source. As soon as they were out of earshot of the cabins, he said, "What do you think you are doing?"

"What are you talking about?" she asked innocently.

"You know exactly what I'm talking about," he said between clenched teeth. "You and Antonine are trying to get Papa and that awful woman married."

Maggie felt a flash of annoyance. "Where do you get off calling Tante names? I thought you had changed since you came here. But you're just as selfish as ever."

Marc stopped in his tracks. He looked surprised. "What on earth are you talking about?"

"You're thinking only about yourself. About whether you want Tante Josephine living in your cabin all the time if she marries your papa. But you're not thinking about him — a poor lonely man. Don't you want him to have someone to share his old age with?"

"And where do you get off thinking you know what's best for other people?"

Marc ran ahead, filled his water bucket and brushed past her without speaking on his way back to his cabin.

That night Madame took Maggie aside and spoke to her quietly.

"I think, my dear Marguerite, that you and Antonine have plans for Tante and Jean-Marc's father."

Maggie felt defensive. "We're just trying to help. Antonine's mother says Tante talks so much to hide her shame of not being married."

"Perhaps so," said Madame slowly. "At least, that may have been the reason when she was a young woman. But now perhaps it is just a habit."

"I don't understand," said Maggie.

"Ah, my dear child!" said Madame. "People complain loudly about Tante and some of her ways, but they don't complain when they need her help. I think she knows that she is needed. I think she has made a place for herself."

"Then you don't think she is unhappy?"

Madame looked thoughtful for a moment before she spoke. "There is something I have noticed in life. Many are given hard lives. But those who live with courage and forget their sorrows by thinking of others, they are the ones who are content."

"But I think Tante is interested in Jean-Marc's papa."

"Perhaps so. But is he interested in her? If you truly respect someone, my child, you trust them to make their own choices."

That was all Madame said. She had spoken softly and lovingly, but Maggie felt chastised far more than when Marc had criticized her. She began to feel ashamed of her interference. Tante would be humiliated if Jean-Marc's papa rejected her. Maggie wished with all her heart that she and Antonine had not started this whole business. But her biggest worry was that now they could not stop what they had started. They had planted an idea in Tante's head, and Tante was not the kind to give up easily.

The next day Tante asked Maggie to accompany her again as she went to minister to Grand-mère, saying that she was sure the child was bringing her good luck. Maggie didn't ask why she needed luck. She was afraid she already knew the answer.

As they walked along the path between the cabins, Tante's voice rattled on, letting the world know that they were coming. Maggie looked ahead and saw Jean-Marc's papa leave his cabin. He seemed to be hurrying, and was just about to disappear around the corner when Tante looked up and saw him.

"Hooeeeee!" she called shrilly. "Wait up, Monsieur, I am bringing something for you."

He stopped in his tracks and his back stiffened. Then slowly, with his head down, he retraced his steps and waited for them at the cabin door. Maggie felt a rush of shame, for now she realized for the first time how miserable her actions had made this shy man.

"Yes, Monsieur. I have brought a bowl of my broth. It will, without a doubt, prove to you that I can cook as well as heal the sick."

"Tante, I thank you," he said politely, but there was no enthusiasm in his voice. "I feel I must say that my mother is an excellent cook as well ..." His voice trailed off lamely.

Grand-mère's face fell when Tante entered the cabin, but

she remembered her manners and asked them to stay for a visit. Tante handed her the bowl of broth.

"I brought this for your son, Madame. I can tell by the look in his eyes that his health is lacking. Oh, he may seem strong to you, to the untutored eye, that is, but an expert like myself can predict what is coming if he doesn't get help soon. He can look forward to rheumatism. Ah yes, the eyes are what tell me these things." Tante Josephine stood directly in front of Papa, staring into his eyes with her face twisted in concentration. Papa turned away.

"I must get back to the fields," he said as if in anguish, and he stepped toward the door.

Tante Josephine moved swiftly and caught his arm. "Oh, but it will take only a moment to drink some of my healing broth. I guarantee that a little of this broth taken everyday will protect you from the rheumatism. Although I must warn you, once you start this treatment, you must not stop. I cannot be held responsible for the deterioration of your health if you should miss taking the potion for even one day."

Papa looked pleadingly at Grand-mère, who was standing by the fire, holding the broth in one hand, her other arm hanging helplessly at her side. When a knock came at the door, she gave the bowl back to Tante and almost ran to answer it.

There, to all their astonishment, stood Robert. "I have come for Tante Josephine," he said, his breaths coming in gasps as if he had run a long way. Then he saw Tante and spoke directly to her. "It is young Madame Aucoin. Her mother sent me to get you. She says there are signs that her daughter will give birth soon. She thinks it may be twins. And it is far too early. She is very worried."

"Twins," said Grand-mère. "When it is twins, we used to say, 'Le Bon Dieu needs two more angels in Heaven.' It is hard to lose your first little ones." The old lady shook her head sadly, as if remembering her own sorrow at losing babies.

"That is an old-fashioned idea!" said Tante Josephine. "I have developed a new method for saving babies that come too soon. It is to keep the child in bed with the mother at all times, for two, even three months. Not every family can spare the mother for that long, so I have allowed an older child, or a grandmother perhaps, to take her place during the day while she goes about her work. It is a matter of keeping the infant as warm as it was in the womb. I have even been successful in saving one of the children from a set of twins this way. Yes, when I attend the birth of such tiny ones, the saying should be changed to, 'Only one angel for heaven; the other for the family.'"

"Then you will come?" asked Robert.

Tante looked at Robert's anxious face, then down at the broth, then at Papa. She hesitated only an instant. Then she handed the bowl to Papa.

"I must go. I am needed more there than here, can't you see? You must understand that I am blessed with a great talent and you will have to get along without me." She took a deep breath, then said, "Come, Robert! We will get my things and leave immediately."

Just before she went out the door, she turned once more to Papa. "Remember, do not drink the broth. It may be a long time until I come this way again, and I wouldn't want to be responsible for its effect. But do not waste it! Feed it to your pig, and I guarantee that it will grow into the biggest, fattest pig you have ever raised."

And with that, Tante Josephine hurried cheerfully up the path, holding Robert's arm and bombarding him with questions about all that had happened at home since she had been away.

Chapter Fifteen

The Accident

Marc and Maggie were so busy that the warm days of July and early August seemed to fly by. They had little chance to talk to each other, but when they did, they didn't mention the whirlpool. Curiously, they seldom worried about it any more. There were many months left before the deportation, and they both felt that somehow they would find it in time.

Each day the sound of axes striking down trees was like a heartbeat as the settlers struggled to claim more land so they could grow more food. There was much complaining about this work, and much longing for the marshes of old Acadia where no trees stood in the way. Not only did they need to grow enough food for their families, but they hoped eventually to produce a surplus from this fertile land to sell to the authorities in Louisbourg, where the land was poor. Then they would have cash to buy things they needed, such as implements for farming and horses and oxen to ease their labour.

One day Jean-Marc's papa was out with his axe, labouring at the edge of the forest. He had left Marc at home stacking firewood by the cabin. Marc was struggling to stack it neatly so that the rows were stable and did not topple over as had happened when he first began the job.

When he heard a commotion, he paused, stick in hand. Monsieur Gallant and his son Benoît were coming toward him, carrying Papa, who was moaning. Marc's heart jumped in his chest when he saw that one of Papa's feet was covered with blood. Then he saw how pale his face was. Even his lips were white.

"His axe slipped," said Monsieur Gallant. "His foot is cut to the bone."

They carried Papa into the cabin and put him on his bed. Grand-mère gave a little cry and stood for a moment with the back of her hand over her mouth. Madame Gallant came rushing in, carrying a length of linen, and the old woman sprang into action, getting a basin of warm water while Madame Gallant began tearing the linen into strips. They shooed Marc outside. First he sat in the dust by the door to wait. Then he realized that Papa would not want him to waste time. He went back to his stacking.

When they called him in, Papa looked as if he was sleeping. The bandages on his injured foot, which was elevated on a pillow of hay, were already bright red.

In the night, Marc woke. Papa was muttering weakly. Grand-mère was sitting beside him. Every few minutes she took a cloth from his forehead, wrung it out in some water, and replaced it. Then her eyes shut and her lips moved in prayer. Marc went to her.

"The bleeding?" he asked.

"It has stopped," she answered. He saw that the foot was freshly bandaged. Papa's face in the flickering candlelight looked different, no longer white.

"He looks better," Marc said.

But by the next night Papa was hot and feverish. Red streaks were stretching up his leg from the injured foot. He opened his eyes and muttered something Marc could not understand. He was delirious. For the first time Marc let himself think the unthinkable.

"Will he die?" Marc asked Grand-mère.

"If Le Bon Dieu wills it."

This can't happen, thought Mark. "Grand-mère, should we send for Tante Josephine?"

"I would if she were free," answered the old lady, "but I know she is busy nursing the children of St. Pierre who are suffering from whooping cough."

Marc's mind was in a turmoil. There must be something he could do to help. He thought of the hospital in Hamilton where he'd spent so many weeks after his accident, and of the doctors and nurses who had saved his life. Then he remembered something he had heard that morning in the field. Monsieur Pitre had returned a few days ago from Port La Joye. He said that a doctor had recently arrived there to treat some of the soldiers who had fallen ill.

"Grand-mère, there is a doctor from Louisbourg over at Port La Joye. Would he come?"

"We will ask the neighbours in the morning if they will go for him. Now go to bed," she said, her voice cracking with exhaustion.

In the morning, Marc decided not to ask a neighbour to ride to Port La Joye for the doctor. They were so busy, and he desperately wanted to handle it on his own. Grand-mère was frightened by the thought of his going so far into the forest by himself, but then she said, "It is important that your father gets help quickly. We can't wait for someone else to go. Ask Monsieur Pitre about the road. And, Jean-Marc, please be careful!"

Monsieur Pitre gave him directions. "You know the path that begins at La Source, then follows the stream. Follow it until it branches away from the stream. There, it joins a road newly cut through the forest. Follow the road until you come to a river. The fording place is marked with piles of stones. When you have crossed, you will see two roads. The one on the right goes to Port La Joye."

Marc hastily bridled Noiraud. The horse blinked sleepily, as if wondering what the rush was about. Marc threw two leather pouches fastened together with a thong across Noiraud's withers and swung onto his bare back. He wished Lkimu was with him. He would know everything about travelling in the forest. Gérard and Joseph waved to him from their field. He called to them as he passed. He was sure that they were looking at him in envy. Before this, only adults had been allowed to go alone on journeys through the forest.

Noiraud had been idle, doing nothing but grazing for several days. He broke into a jerky canter, and Marc hung on for dear life. They found the forest road easily. It was not really a road. The road builders had simply cut a trail through the forest, leaving fallen trees and stumps for travellers to get by as best they could.

Noiraud slowly picked his way, stepping over logs. Hour after hour he plodded on. Marc let the reins dangle against his neck. The sun was above them now, and the horse's dull coat shone with sweat. He pulled his head up sometimes at the whirring of a bird startled into flight, or when an animal rustled through the undergrowth, but as the day wore on, his head hung lower and he seemed not to notice even when a rabbit scurried across the path.

Marc kept thinking about this man he called his father. On the night before his accident, Papa had sat staring into the fire with a sad, faraway look in his eyes. But when Marc came and sat by his knee, he rested his hand on the boy's shoulder and seemed to stir himself from his reverie. Then he began telling Marc stories brought over from France with the first Acadians. After a while, he tucked his fiddle under his chin and filled the little cabin with music. The boy could feel in his spine the thud of Papa's feet beating time on the hard-packed earth floor.

Evening fell and the shadowy forest was becoming cool. Horse and boy drank deeply from a spring at the side of the trail. When they reached the river, Marc dismounted and opened the leather pouches. In one was a few handfuls of barley, the last of the scrapings from the bin in the barn. In the other was the leg of a hare roasted the night before. Marc gnawed strips of meat from the bone. Noiraud was asleep, although still standing. He had only lipped his barley as if he was too tired to eat. Marc wanted to sleep, too, but he thought of Papa and swung onto the horse's back. Daylight was fading but they could travel just a little farther before dark.

At first the old horse refused to enter the river, but when Marc insisted, he gathered himself and plunged in. Water swirled around his hocks, then his knees, then his belly.

"Go, Noiraud. Keep going," Marc urged. Snorting with fear, Noiraud plunged ahead. Then the water began to drop, to his knees then his hocks.

As Noiraud stepped to shore, he suddenly threw back his head, gave a strangled choking sound from far back in his throat and fell to his knees. Marc leaped to the muddy shore as the horse's body sagged and lay still, his hindquarters still in the water.

"Noiraud! Get up. Please!" Marc begged. He put his ear to the horse's nose but could hear no breath. He looked around in panic. He thought of Papa lying helpless in bed. He heard a faraway sound almost like a human scream and he thought of wildcats. It was too dark now to see the roads Monsieur Pitre had described. Sadly, with tears slipping down his cheeks, Marc rubbed his hand along Noiraud's neck.

Marc wished with all his heart that Lkimu was with him. Perhaps he was near; he often seemed to be on his own in the forest. He waited a few minutes, just in case. He even called, "Lkimu," a couple of times in a high, quavering voice. Finally he accepted the fact that he was alone. Absolutely alone.

The safest place to spend the night would probably be in a tree. As he left the river, the sound of running water faded, and again he could hear the squeaks and sighs and rustles of the forest. He found a tree with sturdy spreading branches and climbed until he found a place that would support him in a half-reclining position. He couldn't sleep though, for he was cold, miserable and afraid of falling. Soon all his muscles were stiff and aching. When he thought he couldn't stand the cold and his fear and sorrow any longer, the moon appeared, full and bright. He could see Noiraud's dark form down by the riverbank, and as he looked around, he could clearly make out the two trails.

He decided not to wait for morning; he climbed down and began walking. He walked, he tripped, he got up and walked some more. Dawn came. He came to a part of the road that seemed more frequently used, for it was nearly clear of debris. How long it was taking him! What if Papa died before he returned? He began to run. His feet flew, dodging roots, leaping puddles. A new strength coursed through his body.

Three hours later he was returning along the trail, but now he was seated behind the doctor on the back of a strong, young military horse. His arms were locked around the doctor's waist and his head was lolling against his back. The doctor had recently come to Louisbourg from France, and he had an accent different from the one Marc was now used to.

"You Acadian farmers are a lazy lot," he was saying. "The government sends you over to this island to raise food for Louisbourg, but you send nothing. Instead you constantly beg for help. Your crops are always failing for one reason or another. You must know nothing of good farming practices."

Marc was shocked at the doctor's ignorance. He wanted to tell this arrogant man how hard the people in the settlement worked and how brave they were. But he bit his tongue. Perhaps the doctor could save Papa. That was all that mattered.

"Now, this father of yours is so stupid he mistakes his foot for a tree." The doctor grumbled on while Marc, exhausted from walking and running the night through, dozed fitfully against his back.

When they approached the river, he shut his eyes and kept them shut. He didn't want to see what the wild animals had done to Noiraud. He didn't fully waken until they reached the settlement.

The doctor examined Papa carefully, then turned to Grand-mère. He tilted his head back a little which gave the impression that he was looking down his nose at her as he spoke.

"I'm afraid the infection is spreading," he said. "If the red streaks reach his heart, he will die. I may have to remove the leg."

Marc had watched the doctor pack his case back at Port La Joye. He had seen him put in a small saw. He felt his stomach lurch. He was pretty sure that anesthetic hadn't been invented yet.

Grand-mère gasped, "No!" then covered her mouth with the back of her hand.

"It may be necessary to save his life," said the doctor. "I am going on to the settlement at Havre aux Sauvages now, for there is sickness among the people and several have died. I'll be back in a few days. In the meantime apply this to the wound." He gave Grand-mère a bottle of greasy green salve. "It is my own creation. I'm sure it will help. If not, I will operate when I return."

The doctor went outside with Grand-mère, holding the old woman's trembling arm, telling her in a loud voice how to apply the salve as if he was speaking to someone with inferior intelligence.

"Jean-Marc." It was Papa, his voice barely a whisper. "I heard. They will take my leg."

"Oh, Papa," said Marc, kneeling on the floor beside the bed, feeling helpless.

"Courage, my son," said Papa. "If it will save my life, it must be done. I have prayed for death to end my suffering." He stopped for a moment, gathering his strength. "But I must live for Grand-mère and for you. You have already lost so much. Le Bon Dieu will help me."

He fell into unconsciousness then, and Marc felt warm tears on his cheeks. He didn't bother to wipe them away. He felt a hand on his shoulder. Expecting Grand-mère, he looked up to see Lkimu.

"I just heard," Lkimu said, and he squeezed Marc's shoulder. Then he unwound the bandage and examined Papa's foot and leg. They were now discoloured and swelling badly. "I will bring some medicine," he said, and left.

When Grand-mère came with the jar of salve, Marc put his hand on her arm. "Let's wait for Lkimu," he said. He knew Grand-mère was fond of the people from the Mi'kmaq camp who often shared what they had when food was scarce in the settlement. She sat down and closed her eyes in prayer.

Lkimu was back within the hour, carrying a sack over his shoulder. He flipped it onto the floor beside the bed and took a skin pouch from his waistband. He asked for a cup into which he shook some powder from the pouch. He added a little water which he swirled a few times, raised Papa's head with one arm and held the cup to his lips until he drank. He then lay him back gently and turned his attention to the foot. He removed the bandage, took handfuls of moss from the sack and packed it around the foot and leg. Next he placed strips of birchbark around the moss and fixed it in place with leather thongs. Papa's leg looked like a stout birch log.

For three days Lkimu stayed in their cabin. Whenever Marc came in from the fields, Lkimu was either gently tending the sick man or sitting on the floor by the bed, sometimes with his head slumped forward in sleep. Grand-mère slept better now, knowing that Lkimu would wake when the sick man needed a drink of water, or more of the special potion.

On the second morning he was there, Lkimu was sitting at the table with Marc eating their breakfast of bread and milk. Papa was sleeping. Grand-mère had gone out to work in the garden, saying she wasn't hungry.

Marc had been telling Lkimu about his journey to Port La Joye for the doctor. He told of his night in the tree, and of hearing the screams of an animal.

"Are you ever frightened when you are alone in the forest?" he asked.

Lkimu laughed, then he saw that Marc was serious. "I'm never alone in the forest," he said. "The animals and the trees are with me. Why should I be afraid?" He paused for a moment, then went on more quietly, as if he was suddenly shy. "Something tells me to go there." He rose and went to the window. "Long ago, my people got all they needed from the forest, the rivers and the sea. They didn't eat pea soup and hard buscuits. I would like to be a hunter like my grandfathers before me, but now the game has gone." He stared out the window as he spoke, his fists clenched.

Marc was bewildered. "What do you mean?" he asked. "I know there are animals in the forest."

Lkimu turned and looked at Marc. "Each year the fur-traders take more pelts. There are not as many animals as in the old days." Lkimu returned to his seat at the table, but he didn't touch his food.

Marc was surprised to hear Lkimu talk of "the old days," as if the eighteenth century were modern times. He looked around to make sure Papa was sleeping.

"Lkimu," he said hesitantly, "strange things have happened. I would like to tell you about them." He stopped, not sure how to go on. How could he tell his story of travelling through time, when he could hardly believe it himself? How could he describe his life in the twentieth century so that Lkimu would understand?

"Yes?" said Lkimu expectantly. But Marc was silent.

Both boys were silent for a moment, then Lkimu said quietly, "Sometimes there are things we cannot understand."

"Like the way you can heal people?" asked Marc.

"Yes," agreed Lkimu, "I do not understand this power, but it is good."

"Yes, it is good," said Marc, his voice husky. He got up and went to Papa's bed-side , not able to say more.

On the third day of Lkimu's visit Papa fell into a deep untroubled sleep, his fever gone. The red streaks were fading, and his leg was beginning to return to its normal size. That evening Lkimu left for the Mi'kmaq camp.

Four days later, when the doctor returned, Papa was propped up in bed drinking broth, his foot wrapped in a fresh linen bandage. The doctor examined him carefully.

As he packed his medical bag, he spoke to Grand-mère, shaking his head. "That salve I gave you is a miracle cure, Madame. It has saved your son's leg, and perhaps his life." The old lady said nothing, but Marc could see a little muscle twitching in her wrinkled cheek, as if she was trying not to smile.

As the doctor and his horse disappeared into the forest, Marc went back to work in the fields. He could work for hours now without tiring or getting stiff. His hands had grown tough and didn't blister any more. But it was a memory that gave him strength and joy in his work, the memory of what Papa had said when he began to get well and Grand-mère had told him how Marc had journeyed through the dangerous forest to bring help. Papa had taken Marc's hand in his and said in a weak, halting voice, "You are growing up ... you have proven yourself to be unselfish ... courageous ... You are a true Acadian. I am proud to have you for a son."

Chapter Sixteen

A Plague

While the men continued clearing the land, the women and children scrambled to lay up ammunition to fight their greatest enemy, winter — *l'hiver*. The ammunition consisted of enough clothing to keep their families from freezing and enough food to keep them from starving.

By now, in late summer, all the wool, which was very little, had been carded and spun and woven or knitted into precious warm clothing. But the scramble for food went on. Even the tiniest children could pick berries, although first they had to learn to resist popping them into their hungry mouths. They gave the berries to their mothers who dried them for *l'hiver*. The women and older girls slashed down the wild sweet grass wherever it could be found, and spread it to dry in the sun. Then they loaded it on carts and stored it away for their animals to eat during *l'hiver*.

Madame rationed the bit of wheat that was left and baked only every second day now. The dried peas were gone. Each family picked a cabbage or a turnip daily and put it in the stew pot with a hare or a partridge or whatever else the men might shoot in the little time they had for hunting. With just two guns in the entire settlement, only two men could hunt at a time, and there was little food for the hard-working families.

Sometimes some of the men took their little sailboat out in the Gulf of St. Lawrence and brought back some fish to dry. Fishing was forbidden by the authorities, who thought that the settlers should spend every minute farming and growing food for Louisbourg. So far there hadn't been enough food for the settlers, much less a surplus to send away. So no one felt guilty about catching a few fish to help guard against *l'hiver*. They hid the dried fish as they did their forbidden salt beef under other salted foods in barrels. Hungry as they were, they did not touch this food, because they knew they would be even more hungry in *l'hiver*.

If *l'hiver* was the enemy, there was longing for it, too. By the time it arrived, the fields of grain now rippling in the sea breezes and ripening in the golden sun would be safely stored in bins. There would be flour for loaves of steaming hot bread. The peas would be dried and simmering in the soup pots once more. And, most of all, there would be leisure time to sing and dance and visit with neighbours.

Maggie was tired and her back ached. Last night Madame had found worms in a cabbage and told Maggie she must douse the cabbages with salt water to keep the worms from ruining them. So all morning Maggie had hauled buckets of sea water from the bay. She felt little rivers of sweat running down her back. Her head ached from the hot sun and her heavy clothes. She hated the worms that were eating the precious cabbages. She hated the bucket for being so heavy. She hated the sea for wetting her long skirts so that they stuck clammily to her legs.

She was bending over a cabbage when she heard the yelling. Everyone was looking toward the forest and shouting something.

At first Maggie could see nothing but the black forest. Then her gaze dropped to the ground. A muddy brown line stretched as far as she could see to the left and the right. As she watched, she slowly became aware that it was moving like the tide, bit by bit, a flowing forward here, a pulling back there, but moving all the time. As if her ears had suddenly opened, she finally understood what people were shouting. "*Les souris!* Mice!"

Maggie ran toward the line until she could see hundreds, thousands, maybe millions of mice with round brown bodies and black paws. She could hear a rustling sound, a sound that grew in intensity. It was the sound of chewing. Hundreds of thousands of tiny jaws were gnawing through the stalks of the wild grasses that Isabelle and the other animals needed to live. Mice were swarming into the clearing, methodically eating their way through vegetable gardens. She was enraged. She was still carrying the half-filled bucket. She threw the water at the mice but they didn't even pause in their chewing. One a little ahead of the others scrambled over her bare foot and went on chewing.

Shrieking, Maggie ran to the cabin, her feet flying over the ground. She slammed the door behind her and ran to the window to join the little girls who were watching and squealing. Papa, Madame and the boys were walking toward the cabin, their shoulders slumped. The shovels and hoes that they propped against the cabin were spattered with blood. They came in silently. Jacques watched with the girls at the window. Madame sat at the table with her face in her hands, Papa rubbing her back gently. The others waited at the front window for the army of mice to come into view.

They watched all afternoon. The mice were like a brown flood that swept over the land. The flood moved eventually to the sea. The mice in front were pushed into the water by those pressing from behind, and soon there was a line of drowned mice like a ragged stretch of seaweed along the shore.

The flood of mice had left nothing green in its wake. Fields and gardens were nothing but red soil with sprigs of half-eaten stalks here and there. Every leaf, every tender blade was gone.

"It looks as if a fire swept through," said Papa, standing in the open door.

"*L'hiver*," whispered Madame. "*L'hiver* will still come. Of that we can be sure."

Supper that night was a sinewy old hen, cut in small pieces and stewed with a little barley. Madame added extra water so there would be enough to fill nine bowls.

After the children were in bed, Maggie found she couldn't sleep. Every time she closed her eyes she saw the hordes of mice, and the rustle of their chewing filled her ears. She was very hungry. She thought of how she had freed the bear. It had seemed the right thing to do at the time, but now she realized that she had done a terrible thing to these people who needed meat so badly. Great waves of misery washed over her and she began to cry. The harder she tried to stop, the louder she sobbed.

"Marguerite! What is wrong?" Madame peered anxiously at her. But Maggie only sobbed harder and turned her face into the mattress.

"Here, little one," said Papa. "You will wake your sisters." He scooped her out of bed and carried her like a little child to the fireplace.

"Come here," said Madame, settling into the rocker. Papa put Maggie on her lap, and she pulled Maggie's head to her shoulder. "Ah, my sweet Marguerite," she said. "You are overtired. You think I don't know? You think I've forgotten how hard it is when it is time to leave childhood behind? You work so hard, and you care for your little sisters with kindness and patience. Everyday I thank heaven that I have such a daughter."

Maggie stopped sobbing, the tight feeling in her chest beginning to ease. Madame went on. "You are nearly grown. When I see Antonine so happy, it makes me think that in only a few years you, too, will marry and leave us. It nearly breaks my heart," she whispered into Maggie's neck, "to think of losing you."

Maggie's hand crept up around Madame's neck, then she began crying again.

"What is it?" asked Madame.

"The gardens — the grain — the mice. Oh, how will we be able to live?"

"Do not be afraid, little one," Madame said. "Many times our people have faced hardship, and we have come through — with help from the Blessed Virgin." She looked toward the little carving on its shelf, and her voice became soft and husky. "Pray for strength my child, but do not worry. We will survive."

She began to sing an old Acadian lullaby, her sweet voice strong and comforting. Maggie felt a wonderful calm feeling flooding her body. Safe in Madame's arms, she felt her sobs die away. Madame brushed her calloused hand over Maggie's wet cheeks. "Do you feel better, little one? Can you sleep now?"

"Yes," said Maggie. "Yes, Maman." This last word was very soft, nearly lost in the quiet night sounds of the little cabin. From now on, Maggie knew, she would always think of this woman as Maman.

Maggie crept back to bed. She nestled down between the little girls, relaxed and drowsy. Jeanne turned in her sleep and flung an arm across Maggie's face. Maggie pulled the arm away, but she clung to the thin little hand as she drifted toward sleep. She was still hungry, but another kind of hunger, the kind that for almost as long as she could remember had made her feel lonely and unimportant, had disappeared while she was in that rocking chair.

Chapter Seventeen

A Season of Hope

Marc scooped up some sea water and dribbled it on the back of Maggie's neck. She shrieked and splashed his shirt.

"Take it easy," he shouted. "You'll get my clothes soaked and I'll catch cold or something."

They were gathering mussels along the shore. Wading in the cold water, they tugged the little shellfish from the underside of rocks and tossed them into their buckets. They had volunteered to do this so they could talk. Most of the other children were picking wild fruit.

"You know, I've just noticed something," said Maggie. "We speak French all the time now, even when we're alone."

"I guess it's natural," said Marc. "It's September you know. We've been here more than two months." He spoke vaguely, as if his mind was somewhere else.

"What's the matter, Marc?" asked Maggie, straightening up and looking directly at him.

"I wasn't going to tell you, but I don't think it's right not to."

"Well? What is it?"

"I know where our pine tree is. I saw it near the road when I went to Port La Joye to get the doctor."

Maggie felt a rush of excitement. "What? Oh, Marc! Is the whirlpool there?"

"I didn't have time to look closely, but I could see a dark place on the ground nearby."

"Why didn't you tell me?"

"It sounds silly, but everyone's been having such a hard time, I'm not sure it would be right to leave right now. Does that make any sense to you?"

Maggie knew exactly what he meant. She was happy to know that the whirlpool was there for when they needed it, but she wasn't ready to leave her Acadian family now, not just yet. She was not anxious to give up being part of Marguerite's warm, loving family. Not when she remembered all her sad years without one.

"I miss my real parents," Marc went on. "But I don't want to leave here until Papa has his strength back."

"When do you think we should go?"

"You know that the villagers have asked Louisbourg to send food. Jean-Baptiste is afraid that we won't survive the winter without it. We could go after the food comes. Grand-mère says Papa will be better in a few weeks."

"Okay, when the food comes. It's a deal!"

Maggie had another reason to stay in the settlement a little longer. Antonine was leaving soon to spend the winter in St. Pierre. Tante Emilie was ill and needed her help.

Maggie threw her arms around Antonine when she found she was leaving. "I don't want you to go," she said in a choking voice. "But I know you must. I promise you one thing: I'll never forget you, no matter what."

126

"You silly girl," Antonine laughed. "You cry as if we are parting forever. I'll be back in the spring. Then you can help me plan for my wedding. And you will meet my Étienne!"

"Of course," moaned Maggie, struggling to control her tears. "You are right, of course. When I feel sad, I promise that I will think of you being near your dear Étienne and I will be happy because you are happy."

The day Antonine left with her father in one of the canoes, Maggie remembered her promise and she did not cry.

Many weeks passed, and the food did not come from Louisbourg. November came with cold winds and gray days and still the food didn't come. The settlers stayed in their cabins now, except when they were hunting or tending their animals. They considered the amount of fodder already stored before the plague of mice had destroyed the crops, and calculated how many animals could survive the winter. They made plans to slaughter the rest for food even though they were breeding stock, and without them there would be no baby animals in the spring.

Just before Christmas some soldiers with a dozen pack-horses arrived in the village. A ship had come from Louisbourg to Port La Joye, and parties of soldiers were distributing supplies to the settlements suffering from famine. Everyone crowded around as they unloaded sacks of dried peas and flour and kegs of molasses. Jean-Baptiste and the other men distributed the food according to the number of people in each household.

"Do they expect us to live all winter on this?" asked Maman, surveying the few sacks on the cabin floor.

"We must ration it carefully. Now, don't be sad," Papa said, taking her chin in his hand. "I have good news from a soldier. He told me the priest who is chaplain at Port La Joye will visit us at Christmas time."

"Oh! Oh!" was all Maman said. But her smile came back and her shoulders straightened a little.

Maggie and Marc agreed they would not leave just yet. With pea soup bubbling in the pots once more, even if it was watery, and with Christmas coming soon, there was a hopeful spirit in the little settlement.

"Besides," Maggie told Marc, "I don't think it would be a lot of fun jumping into the whirlpool at this time of year."

Marc readily agreed that spring would be a better time.

At midnight on Christmas Eve the entire community gathered at Jean-Baptiste's, and the priest celebrated Mass. In the corner of the room, glimmering darkly in the shadows, was the bell, the symbol of hope for a prosperous future with a real church and a priest of their own. Maman knelt with her family. Her face was shining with joy in the soft light of candles.

Christmas Day was unlike any Maggie and Marc had ever known. There was no tree, no special feast, no mention of Santa Claus or Father Christmas. In the afternoon everyone was called back to Jean-Baptiste's to receive a gift.

All the people from the settlement crowded into Jean-Baptiste's cabin. They were curious and excited about the prospect of a gift for the whole community. Beside Jean-Baptiste, at the head of the table was an old Mi'kmaq woman. She wore a mixture of clothing styles. On her head was a pointed headdress, quite different from the white caps worn by the Acadian women. But she wore a dress, and over it layers of shawls. Just showing, under the hem of her dress, were mocassins decorated with colourful beadwork.

Jean-Baptiste, as always the spokesman for the Acadians, turned to the wrinkled old woman and said, "We wish to thank you, Madame Florentine. We thank you and your people for your help in these hard times. Often, when we have been near despair, you and our many Mi'kmaq friends have shown us kindness. You have helped us survive many plagues. Now, you bring us a gift to celebrate Christmas, and we thank you for that as well."

On the table in front of them was a crèche made from woven twigs and birchbark, displayed on a bed of spruce boughs. The Christ child, a tiny figure of carved wood, rested in a manger lined with fur. He was covered with a blanket of soft leather intricately embroidered with tiny beads. Adults moved back from the table so the children could come near. Some hoisted small children up so they could see over the heads of the other children. A hush fell over the room as they gazed at the tiny figure.

Maggie led Françoise and Jeanne forward so they could see. She knelt between them. They were almost holding their breath. Little Jeanne reached out a finger and touched the tiny fur robe.

"Pretty," she whispered.

"Yes," said Maggie, feeling a sense of wonder and joy surrounding her. "Yes," she repeated softly, "yes, it is wonderful."

Winter arrived with a fierce snowstorm on the first day of the new year, 1758. It was to be a winter of storms. Often when Maggie looked from the front window she could not see the animal shed through the whirling whiteness. The family moved slowly and spoke little, trying to conserve their strength. Maggie thought that what she missed most was Papa's booming laugh, which used to ring out so often, making everyone around him smile.

Maggie shivered and pulled her shawl closer around her shoulders. All summer she had complained of the discomfort of wearing heavy woollen garments, but now she gladly put on extra layers of petticoats, a woollen jacket and thick stockings. She wore moccasins now, indoors as well as out. Still she was cold. The wind blew through cracks on every side of the cabin and the drinking water froze in the bucket. The fire burned constantly, but she could feel the heat only when she was directly in front of it. Only at night was she warm. Snuggled between Jeanne and Françoise, wrapped in layers of underwear and with the wool blankets pulled to her chin, she felt the cold seep from her bones and she dreamed of hot air puffing from the registers in the house on George Street and of eating a giant pepperoni pizza.

One day Papa left the cabin early. He returned for the noon meal. Maggie knew he was back when she heard him stamping the snow from his moccasins before he opened the door.

The family sat down to eat. Maman had divided the remains of yesterday's loaf into nine equal pieces spread with butter and molasses. Each tin cup was only half-filled with milk, for Isabelle was producing little on her scanty winter rations.

"What is the matter, Papa?" asked Jeanne, after they had given thanks for their food.

"I have just been to see how the refugees around the point are getting along in this bitter weather," he said. "They have food, as we do, from Louisbourg, but they don't have enough clothing. Those who have no shoes have nothing but rags to wind around their feet. They are very sick. I'm afraid many will die before spring if they don't get help. I'm asking around the community to see if each person can contribute something, no matter how little." He paused and looked down the table at his children. "Do you think we have anything we can spare?"

For a moment there was silence as every pair of hungry eyes looked at Papa. Then Maman stood up. She took her jacket from where it hung on a wooden peg in the wall near the door. It was the new one that Maggie had helped sew.

"Of course we have things to share," Maman said. "Here, take this jacket. I still have the old one. I don't need two!" She folded it and laid it on the chair by the fire.

Papa got up and brought back his newest mittens, the ones without any mends, and a warm, woollen shirt. He put them on the jacket. Jacques unwound the scarf from his neck, and each of the boys added something to the pile, a pair of socks or mittens.

Maggie looked at Jeanne and Françoise. All three girls looked toward their cozy bed. The top blanket was a bit tattered, but there was much warmth in it. Maggie removed it, slowly folded it and added it to the other things.

"There now," said Papa with something of his old cheerfulness. "I am proud of you all."

The winter was very long and many were sick, but everyone survived. With spring came rushing ice-water streams, buds on the trees and flocks of returning birds filling the sky.

One warm spring day Marc was on the shore with Gérard and Joseph.

"Look!" he said pointing. "A ship." It was anchored a long way out and a boat was pulling toward them.

"Perhaps it's from France, coming to catch our fish," said Joseph. But when the boat pulled to shore, they found it carried seed grain from Louisbourg.

"Get along, young fellows, and get your fathers down here to help us unload these sacks," shouted a sailor. "Either you move fast, or we'll dump it overboard to feed the fishes!" He made a move to pick up a sack.

"Wait," shouted Gérard. "We'll get them!" And the three boys ran toward the cabins, shouting.

The spirit came back to the people then. Weak as they were, they began preparing the fields for planting the peas and the wheat. By early summer they were able to add some fresh vegetables and the first berries to their diet. Once again it was a season of hope.

Chapter Eighteen

War!

By July the crops were tall in the fields. The few hens kept in the settlement during the long winter had hatched chickens. Once again chicks scratched around the stumps. Isabelle's ribs no longer showed, and her coat had lost its dull look. She grazed day after day on lush summer grass with a new calf at her side.

One evening, when the day's work was done, Joseph ran through the settlement shouting, "A meeting! A meeting now at the home of Jean-Baptiste."

People poured from their cabins, some carrying children already asleep. There was a growing buzz of voices as they approached the large cabin.

"What is it?"

"Have you heard anything?"

"I think it has something to do with the war."

"Will the wars between France and Britain never end?"

"I pray that Jean-Baptiste brings us a message of peace."

They gathered in front of Jean-Baptiste's cabin, some sitting on stumps, some leaning against the rail fence, others standing. Marc caught Maggie's eye. They both knew that what they dreaded most was about to happen.

"My friends," said Jean-Baptiste from his front step. "I have just returned from Port La Joye with news of the war. Louisbourg has fallen to the British." He waited until the buzz of voices died down. "And worse news. The British plan to deport us, to send us away from our homes. Away from our island. I think the soldiers will be coming soon."

Marc stood behind the stump on which Grand-mère was sitting. She began to tremble. The winter had been particularly difficult for her. She began to sob, covering her eyes with her hands. Marc wanted to comfort her, but he wasn't sure how. All he could do was pat her shoulder clumsily. She made an effort to control her weeping, bunching her clean white apron with her gnarled fingers. Gradually she quieted.

"Grand-mère is right to weep." It was Marguerite's maman, her voice shrill. "Soldiers, even French soldiers, care nothing for us, the people. They know only war and fighting over colonies for their greedy kings. Who fights for the people?"

"Who fights, indeed?" said Jean-Baptiste, his voice weary. "You and I would fight, my friends." His eyes swept the scene and fell on Jacques, Joseph and Marc. "I'm sure even our children would fight for the right to build our church, to live in peace. But we are too weak. We cannot fight the kings of Europe with their wealth, their soldiers, their ships and their guns."

"What can we do then?" asked Monsieur Gallant.

"As I see it, we have two choices," said Jean-Baptiste. "We can go quietly with the British soldiers. Or we can hide from them in the forest."

"What will you do?" someone shouted.

Jean-Baptiste straightened his shoulders. The sadness in his face was replaced with a look of determination. "Île St. Jean is my home," he said. "My family and I will stay. We will find a hiding place. I invite all of you to join us."

Monsieur Gallant pushed his way to the front of the crowd. "You are losing your senses, old man. Without food or shelter you ask us to face winter? In the midst of this short summer, have you forgotten the cold and hunger? You are counselling death."

Many muttered in agreement.

Marc was upset. He knew things that these people didn't know. He felt obliged to speak, though he was afraid his words wouldn't be taken seriously because he was young.

"With respect, Monsieur Gallant," he said politely but firmly, "you are forgetting our friends the Mi'kmaq. They bring us food and medicine. They can hide us in the forest where the soldiers can never find us."

Many people nodded in agreement.

Then Marguerite's papa leaped to his feet. "How long could we hide? We are farmers. Would the British allow us to farm? I say there is nothing left for us here."

Some of the people agreed with one speaker, some with another. They began arguing with those next to them. Jean-Baptiste held up his hand.

"What makes you think the British will keep Île St. Jean? Acadia has changed hands many times, from French to British and back. Now the British have the upper hand, but next year? Who knows."

Gérard spoke then. "You all seem to think there are two possibilities. We should hide and starve in the woods, or we should allow ourselves to be herded onto filthy ships like sheep. I refuse to be treated like an animal — or a criminal. There are boats on our shores. The St. Lawrence River leads like a highway to freedom."

"Ha!" shouted his father. "You think you are a sailor now? A bunch of farmers crowded into the few small boats? How many of us could survive out there on the open water? Even if we could survive the sea, we would still be in danger. The Gulf of St. Lawrence is probably crawling with British ships."

The meeting broke up in disarray. Marc walked home with Maggie.

"What are you going to do?" she asked in a tight voice.

"Papa and Grand-mère say they will wait here for the deportation," he said. "They're not strong enough to do anything else. What about you and your family?"

"We're going to wait for the British, too. Papa says the little children would not survive a winter in the forest."

Marc was silent. He was thinking of the whirlpool. He was sure she was, too. They had always said they would return to their own century before this terrible thing happened. But now that it was at hand, everything seemed so much more complicated.

"It's not just duty," said Maggie, as if she had to explain. "I don't want to disappoint Maman and Papa and the younger children by running out on them now when we need each other most."

Marc could tell from her voice just how much Maggie loved her Acadian family. It was different for him. He respected Papa and Grand-mère and cared deeply for their welfare. But his feelings were not as strong as those he had for his real parents.

"Marc, are you scared?"

"Well, to be honest, yeah, of course I'm scared. Aren't you?"

"Yes, sure, but I mostly feel sad."

"We know what's going to happen," said Marc. "There should be some way we can help."

"I've been thinking a lot about this. Everything has already happened. It's in the history books. It's impossible for us to change anything."

"But we're living now. The history books haven't been written yet!"

Maggie touched his hand for a moment before she continued quietly. "I can't explain it, but I'm sure that all we're doing is observing, seeing things. Just think. If we had the power to change anything, all these people, all of us, would have enough food and clothes."

Marc sighed. "I know you're right. I was just hoping you could see some way out. I can't."

The next day, word came from Port La Joye that the deportation order was being appealed by the French authorities. The people in the settlement waited.

Word came, finally, that the appeal had been rejected. Even though the news was bad, there was a strange feeling of relief in the settlement. Now at least the waiting was over and the people could prepare to meet their fate.

Chapter Nineteen

Marc's Decision

That night, when it was dark and the villagers were sleeping, something woke Marc. He lay in his narrow bed holding his breath, listening. He could hear Papa snoring. Grand-mère, who slept near the fire, was muttering. Then he heard again what had wakened him — an owl hooting. But it was an unnatural hoot, too close, too muted. Marc slipped out of bed, pulled on his clothes and went outside.

It was a dark night with the moon hidden behind clouds. He stood in front of the cabin wondering what to do next when he felt a hand on his arm and someone murmured into his ear. Then he was led away.

It was Gérard who was guiding him past a field of peas, to the top of the bank, then down to the shore. Finally they could talk, but they still spoke in muffled voices. Marc recognized the voices of Gérard's brother, Joseph, and Marguerite's brothers, Jacques, Pierre and Charles.

"We're leaving tonight — now," said Gérard. "Will you come with us?"

As he spoke, the clouds thinned and the darkness was

suddenly less dense. But the air was still murky with fog, and it was still impossible to see anything clearly. Marc could make out the hazy shape of one of the larger Mi'kmaq canoes in front of him.

"We're going up the St. Lawrence," said Gérard.

"In that?" asked Marc.

"No. The Mi'kmaq will take us out into the gulf. A French schooner is waiting tonight. It will be picking up people from other settlements, too."

Marc's mind was a whirl of conflicting thoughts. He knew from the history books that some Acadians escaped the deportation by fleeing to Quebec. But he wasn't an expert in history. There was much he didn't know. Gérard and Joseph's father had said that the gulf was full of British ships. Perhaps these young men would be captured. What would happen to them then? This was a time of war, and he suspected prisoners would be treated badly. Would they be punished for trying to escape the deportation? he wondered. Maybe they would be killed. He was frightened.

And yet his heart was nearly bursting with excitement. The young men now clambering into the canoe were his friends. They were full of daring. He could feel their excitement. This was the adventure of their lives. And they wanted him to go with them. They expected him to go. He turned and looked back toward his cabin. In his mind's eye, he could see the embers of the evening fire glowing in the fireplace. He could hear the soft snores of the kind old lady and the louder snores of the man who had given him the most important lesson of his life — the will to live through pain and loss with courage and honour. He paused for a long moment, wanting to go with his friends, yet wanting to stay. He took a deep breath, waded out to the canoe and climbed in.

Four Mi'kmaq were in the canoe. Marc sat behind one of them. He could see the outline of shoulders, head and arm. The figure turned around, reached out a hand and said, "Jean-Marc." It was Lkimu. Then, with powerful thrusts of the paddles, the canoe began moving swiftly and silently through the water. Charles began to speak, but one of the Mi'kmaq admonished him sharply. From then on they were all silent. Marc wondered how the Mi'kmaq knew where they were going in the dark.

Gérard sat next to Marc. He touched Marc's arm and leaned toward him, pointing dead ahead. At first Marc thought it was a little star on the horizon, shining then fading, then shining again. Then he remembered that the stars were not visible. The light was small and hazy through the thin fog. It must be some kind of signal.

The light died. The canoe stopped. The Mi'kmaq had their paddles in the water, but only to keep the canoe from drifting with the tide. Had something happened to the schooner they were headed for? Marc wanted to ask, but didn't dare make a sound.

He felt the canoe rising and falling. There was a creaking and groaning. The canoe rocked more violently. Then Marc heard a voice.

"All clear starboard, Cap'n." The voice was speaking in English!

A ship loomed out of the mists. It looked immense to those in the canoe. It was only about twenty metres away and high above them in the water. Marc could barely make out the shape of a sail, but he could hear several voices and they were all speaking English, not loudly, but clearly on the night air.

Marc held his breath, his heart beating wildly. Then, with a groan of wood rubbing on wood and the creak of a mast, the boat moved from their path.

Marc thought that the Mi'kmaq were waiting until the wash had died before they began paddling again. But the sea grew calmer and still they waited. He was getting cold. And still they waited. Then he saw the tiny signal light, one more time, and the canoe was off, streaking through the water.

Minutes later Marc could make out another ship, much smaller than the last, and he knew it must be the French schooner they were looking for. The canoe pulled beside it and one of the Mi'kmaq called out. In a moment the end of a rope was tossed into the canoe. Charles was the first to be pulled aboard, then Joseph. Marc knew it would be his turn in a minute, and he suddenly felt unsure. Was he doing the right thing? When Papa and Grand-mère woke in the morning and found him gone, what would they think? How would they get along without him? He knew that their friends would try to help them, but they had their own families to worry about. He had to decide now. He began to panic.

Marc touched Lkimu on the arm. "What should I do?" he asked.

Lkimu turned to him. "It is for you to decide," he said. His calm voice steadied Marc. He felt stronger and more sure of himself.

As Pierre climbed over the side of the schooner, Marc grabbed Gérard's arm.

"I'm not going with you," he said.

Gérard sounded astonished. "I don't understand. Why?"

"It's Papa. He hasn't got his strength back yet. He won't be able to look after Grand-mère without my help. I want to go with you, but I've got to go back."

"Hurry up!" someone said.

Marc sat back down in the boat.

Gérard paused a moment. "I'm sorry you're not coming. When we meet again, we'll have a lot to talk about." Then he grabbed the rope, and without another word he was gone. As Marc moved to a new sitting place in the centre of the canoe in front of Lkimu, the sky was beginning to get lighter.

The canoe turned toward the shore and home. Marc looked back at the schooner only once and felt a sharp sense of loss. It was already disappearing, taking his friends with it, fading like a ghost ship into the morning mists.

Chapter Twenty

Secret Places

In mid-August some Mi'kmaq came to the settlement to tell the settlers that one of the British commanders, Lord Rollo, had sailed to Port La Joye with four warships. There, some of his men were at work building a new British fort, while others were being dispatched across the island to round up the Acadians for deportation.

As the days and weeks passed, news of the deportation dribbled in bit by bit; groups of Acadians from other parts of the island had already been shipped away, but the Mi'kmaq didn't know their destination. They said that the British soldiers were burning the abandoned crops and the buildings in the settlements. The soldiers didn't want to leave anything behind in case the French came back after the war. The Mi'kmaq also said that some of the younger and stronger people had escaped to the mainland, where they hoped to make homes in the wilderness.

It was time to harvest the grain and dry the peas. Some of the settlers argued that since the soldiers would be coming soon, there was no point in a harvest. But the thought of losing all that good food was too much to endure for people who had so recently lived with hunger. So they harvested their crops.

In the evening, when the work was done, Jeanne and Françoise asked about their brothers.

"They are far away, in a safe place," said Papa.

"I want Jacques to carry me on his shoulders," said Jeanne.

"When we see Jacques again, you will be too big for him to carry you," said Maman.

Maman's eyes were red sometimes. Then Maggie knew that she had been weeping for her lost sons. But whenever Maman and Papa talked, they spoke of how happy they were that at least some of the family had escaped. "I'm sure they are safe," each said to the other.

In October, when all the harvesting was done and the dried peas were in sacks, five young Mi'kmaq emerged from the forest. They said that a party of soldiers was headed toward the village.

The Mi'kmaq also said that since the harvest the soldiers had decided not to burn the wheat and peas when they came. They were planning to come later with boats and take the crops and the animals for their own use.

The Mi'kmaq had formed a new plan. They would hide in the woods waiting for the soldiers to leave with their captives. Then they would come out of the forest, take what they could carry, then destroy what was left. Better to burn the food than let the enemy get it, they said.

Jean-Baptiste called all the families to one last meeting. This time, instead of meeting at his cabin, he asked them to meet in the forest, near La Source. He also asked them to bring any valuables that they wanted to hide.

They gathered in a dry spot not far from La Source. There, in the ground, was a pit about two metres deep and a little more than two metres in diameter. With the settlers grouped around, their heads bowed in sadness, Jean-Baptiste and Marguerite's papa set the church bell on the bottom of the hole.

"We will return," Jean-Baptiste said solemnly, as if he was officiating over a grave. "One day we will return to our farms. Then we will build our church." He raised his eyes to look at the people, and his voice grew strong. "I promise you, my friends! This bell, which we have cherished for so long, will one day be in its rightful place in the steeple of our church! We will not forget our dreams."

Then, family by family, the people put their valuable possessions in the pit. Madame Gallant carefully laid down the crèche, the only gift given on what, for Maggie, had been the most memorable Christmas of her life. It had been packed lovingly in a small wooden box made for it by Jean-Marc's papa. He had also built a wooden case to protect his most precious possession, his fiddle.

Maman, with tears in her eyes, gently laid the little Virgin, wrapped carefully in a sheet of linen, beside the bell. Others came forward and deposited various bundles and boxes. When they had finished, Jean-Baptiste and some of the other men covered the precious objects, first with soil, then with leaves and rocks.

A few Mi'kmaq men waited at the edge of the forest while Jean-Baptiste, with his family at his side, said farewell to everyone.

"We will meet again," he said, but his voice broke when he said it.

Marguerite's papa shook Jean-Baptiste's hand. "Goodbye, old friend," he said. "Thank you for all you have done for us. I promise you, no matter how far they take us, we will never forget our friends and this beautiful land that has become our home."

The Mi'kmaq led Jean-Baptiste and his family into the forest.

"Where are they taking them?" Maggie asked Papa.

"To some far and secret place," he answered, his voice husky. "I'm not sure where. Jean-Baptiste told me this morning that several families from other parts of the island are already in hiding, and he and his family will join them."

The people turned then, as if in a collective daze, and drifted back toward their homes. To wait. As they waited, they watched clouds of smoke on the horizon, billowing up from far-off burning villages. Maggie knew that, as they watched, they were thinking of something else being destroyed. They were thinking of their dreams wafting upward in those clouds of smoke, upward into the sky.

Chapter Twenty-one

The Deportation

A day later thirteen red-coated British soldiers arrived at the settlement. Maggie had been fearing their arrival for so long that she expected them to look like monsters. Surprisingly, they looked like perfectly ordinary young men, but they all carried guns and that frightened her. They spoke freely in front of the settlers, not realizing that Maggie and Marc could understand what they were saying. Well, most of what they were saying. The soldiers had an unfamiliar accent and used words that they didn't recognize.

There didn't seem to be a commanding officer present. At least to Marc and Maggie's eyes, there weren't any clues in the uniforms to designate different ranks. But one of the soldiers took command and began to order the others about. He divided them into three parties. A group of seven were ordered to haul the grain, flour and peas down to the shore. Maggie heard them talking about a boat that would be arriving soon to take the food as well as the animals to help feed the British troops.

Four other soldiers were given the job of herding the settlers down the road to Port La Joye, where boats were waiting to take them across the ocean to France. The last group consisted of only two soldiers, a pasty-faced young man and the one who was in charge. They leaned against the corral fence, telling jokes and laughing at their companions lugging heavy loads to the shore. Their job was to burn the cabins and the sheds. They must destroy everything, they said, so that there would be nothing left in case the enemy French one day regained control of the island.

Maggie was walking with her Acadian family through the forest when she heard the roar of the fires. Like the others, she couldn't resist turning and looking. The settlement was already hidden from view, but she could see billows of smoke through a screen of tree branches. The soldiers behind them gestured with their guns and shouted at them to keep going.

Maman said quietly, through clenched teeth, "Don't give them the satisfaction of seeing you cry." She took Maggie's hand and they marched straight ahead, their hearts aching but their eyes dry. Maggie was glad that the village was hidden by the forest. She didn't want to see the destruction of the little cabin where she had learned about courage, sharing and love.

It took two days of hard marching to reach Port La Joye. The villagers were exhausted when they arrived, even the strong ones who had to help the children and the old and weak. They also had the added burden of carrying small bundles of their clothing and bedding, all they were allowed to bring. Those who had no shoes arrived with their feet bleeding from the rough forest road. Marc walked between his papa and Grand-mère, his strong young arms linked with theirs. He carried their belongings in a pack on his back.

When the little band arrived at Port La Joye, they found the place in chaos. Other rag-tag groups of Acadians were being brought in, some by land, some by boat. Hundreds of people milled around. One large log building looked brand new, and several others were in various stages of construction. The red, white and blue striped British flag was flying above the large building. This was no longer Port La Joye, Marc whispered to Maggie. It was the new British fort that Lord Rollo's men had been constructing since they had first arrived in August.

Madame Gallant was walking with her husband and children just ahead of Maggie's family. Suddenly she broke away from the group and ran toward a young Acadian woman standing with her back to them. The young woman turned her head just far enough for Maggie to see a rosy cheek and unruly light-brown curls escaping from her cap. Maggie's heart skipped a beat and she stopped still.

"Antonine!" shouted Madame Gallant. The young woman turned toward her. She was not Antonine. A soldier waved his gun at Madame Gallant and shouted at her. She meekly returned to her place, sobbing bitterly. Maggie's eyes darted from face to face, looking for Antonine, but she recognized no one in the milling crowd. Then she remembered that hundreds had already been deported over the past weeks. It was unlikely that Antonine would be there at the same time as she was.

Three ships were in the harbour, their white sails like sea gulls hovering in the blue sky. Several rowboats, with English sailors at the oars, were pulling away from shore toward the ships. Each boat was crammed with Acadians holding their bundles, their children and each other.

"Which ship are you from?" shouted a soldier to a sailor in a boat preparing to load.

"The *Narcissus*," the sailor shouted back.

The soldier began pushing and prodding Acadians toward the boat with the butt of his gun. People scrambled into the water. Mothers and fathers held the hands of children and hauled them upright when they stumbled and fell.

Jean-Marc's papa held Grand-mère's arm with both his hands as they slowly made their way toward the boat, the water swirling around their feet, then their ankles, then their legs before they were roughly hauled aboard. Behind them, Françoise fell in the water and began to cry. Papa swept her in his arms and carried her. Maman held the hands of Jeanne and Michel.

As Maggie and Marc were about to follow the others toward the boat, a sailor shouted, "All full," and lowered his oars into the water.

The soldier behind Maggie and Marc shouted, "Next boat." He pointed with his gun toward another boat already loading a little way down the beach. Marc slipped the pack from his back and shouted to his papa. A soldier took the pack and waded out and threw the pack into the boat, which was already starting to pull away.

"Marguerite!" Maman shouted.

"Maman. Do not worry," she shouted back. "Jean-Marc and I will watch out for each other."

"Which ship are you from?" the soldier shouted to the sailors in the boat that was loading down the beach. "The *Duke William*," one answered.

Marc looked sharply at Maggie. "Don't get in," he whispered. He looked around, as if searching for a way to escape.

Soldiers were herding Acadians toward the boat. In a group just ahead of Marc and Maggie, a young man, after looking hurriedly around, suddenly shot out his fist, catching the soldier who was nearest him on the side of the head. Stunned, the soldier slumped forward, his rifle sliding from his hands. The Acadian snatched the rifle and whirled around to face those coming behind him. The soldier who was herding Marc and Maggie gave a cry. He and a dozen other British soldiers raised their guns to their shoulders and pointed them at the

Acadian, but the young man, trembling, refused to lower his weapon.

They all stood stock still, facing each other like statues for what seemed like minutes. From where they were standing, Marc and Maggie could see what the young rebel could not. Another soldier was slowly working his way behind him. Maggie held her breath, her heart thumping, as the soldier slowly raised his gun high over the young Acadian's head, then with all his strength, brought the butt down, knocking him unconscious.

There was a sudden buzz of voices. Marc and Maggie looked around. They were now at the rear of the crowd with all eyes turned toward the scene of hopeless defiance. Maggie motioned to Marc but he was already walking backward. She followed, and by the time the excitement was over, they were in the shadow of the new log building.

They sidled along the wall, expecting at any moment to be spotted. In her imagination Maggie heard a shout go up and saw hordes of soldiers pointing their rifles at her and Marc. But, no, the crowd on the shore continued loading the boats, with their faces to the sea. In the confusion no one had missed them.

Behind the building, a strip of meadow separated them from the forest. The forest, which they knew was full of danger. Where would they go? How could they possibly survive on their own?

Maggie turned to Marc. "I think we might have been better off taking our chances on the boat."

"Not on that boat," said Marc. "That boat, the *Duke William*, is in the history books. It sank on the way to France and everyone drowned."

Just then a shadow detached itself from the other shadows of the forest. It was Lkimu beckoning to them.

Chapter Twenty-two

The Whirlpool

The three of them ran through the forest. Marc and Maggie, more clumsy than Lkimu, kept catching their clothes on branches. They stumbled over rocks and scratched their skin on bushes. Lkimu was like the wind, dodging here and there, finding a path without slackening his pace. At last they stopped and rested.

When they had caught their breath, Marc asked, "Lkimu, what's going to happen to us?"

"I can't tell you that," said Lkimu. He seemed sad. He took them to a spring where they drank and he gave them strips of dried meat to chew. They went on for a time through the forest, walking now, until they came to a shore. Lkimu pulled a small canoe from its hiding place under an overhanging bank and they got in.

With a quick thrust of his paddle, they were off. The canoe skimmed across the water, kilometre after fleeting kilometre down a river, deep into the forest. Night fell, and they beached the canoe. Lkimu showed them how to burrow into a pile of leaves, their backs to a log. He slept instantly and deeply. Soon

Marc and Maggie dozed, though the cold of the October night woke them many times.

With the first light they were off again, walking quickly in single file with Lkimu in the lead. When Maggie felt she must rest or collapse, Lkimu suddenly stopped and turned.

"I must leave you here."

"Lkimu," said Marc, "I don't want you to go."

The Mi'kmaq boy put his hand out and touched Marc's arm. His long black hair partly covered his face so Maggie couldn't see his expression.

"I'm sorry, Jean-Marc. But you must find your own way now, as I've found mine. I'll never forget you. Perhaps, somehow, we'll meet again."

Before Marc and Maggie could say anything more, he disappeared behind a spruce tree.

They ran a few steps after him, but he was gone.

"What did he mean by that?" asked Maggie. "About him finding his own way? He always seemed to know where he was going."

"It was just some stuff we talked about once," said Marc. "I think he meant that things are working out for him."

"He didn't even give us a chance to say goodbye," said Maggie. For a moment, Marc gazed silently at the spot where Lkimu had disappeared, then he turned to Maggie. "It looks as if we're on our own. Do you have any idea where to go from here?"

They scanned their surroundings. Thick forest surrounded them. Maggie looked up. She could see a patch of sky and some fragments of white clouds drifting across it. Then she saw it.

"Look, Marc." She pointed to a soaring tree, its tip pointing like a giant finger to the heavens. Then they both understood.

They fought their way through the underbrush until they stood at the foot of the pine tree. In front of them, yawning at its base, was a large round hole. They looked over the edge.

Black water swirled like bath water going down a drain. They leaned forward to get a better look, beginning to feel mesmerized by the swirling.

Maggie reached out and took Marc's hand. They looked up once. A blue jay flashed its wings and settled on a branch of the pine. Something rustled and rippled through the undergrowth and was gone.

"If that's you, Lkimu, thank you," said Maggie.

"I'll never forget you, Lkimu," said Marc softly. Something tight in his voice made Maggie look at him. He was staring down at his feet and his cheeks were wet. "Let's go," he said thickly.

Still holding hands, they jumped.

Maggie expected to sink under the water, then to pop up again as she did when she dived into a pool. But her hand was torn from Marc's and she plummeted down and down until she felt an immense pressure.

When she thought she was certain to drown, her face broke surface. There was Marc beside her. They blinked until they could see. They were in the cave. They were wearing orange life jackets over their shirts and bathing suits.

"It's the same as when we left," Maggie said amazed. "But we were away for months."

"Two summers, one winter," Marc said, looking around the walls of the cave. "Look at how high the shelf is," he said. "I'll bet the tide's going out."

They waited, treading water. Soon they could see a glimmer of light. The light grew. When they were sure it was the opening, they swam to it and, holding the edge, ducked their heads and pulled themselves out into the bay.

The sun was shining and the water was calm. They found their canoe washed up on the bank. It looked unharmed, but both paddles were missing. They pulled it into the water.

Marc hauled and rolled himself into it. Maggie suddenly realized his legs were gone. She sighed. She remembered Marc running on the beach. She remembered him dancing, his head thrown back as he laughed with pleasure. She remembered how he ran through the forest to get help for his papa.

Marc saw the look on her face. "Don't worry about me. I knew this would happen when I jumped."

"But you jumped anyway," said Maggie.

"I thought about my … papa," said Marc quietly, not looking at her. "He was ready to lose his leg. He didn't complain or feel sorry for himself because he was thinking of Grandmère and me. While he was sick, I thought a lot about how Mom and Dad must have felt when I had my accident. I gave them a hard time. I want to see my parents again."

Maggie waded a few metres out, following the shoreline in hip deep water, pulling the canoe along beside her. In a couple of places the water was so deep that she had to swim a little, always guiding the canoe with one hand.

They had been silent for a long time, both thinking, remembering.

"I wonder why," Marc said.

"Maybe they were your ancestors," said Maggie.

"Probably, but you heard the voice first. I wonder why."

They were silent again for a few minutes. "This is the same bay. The same bay where the village was," Maggie said. "I'm sure it is although it does look different."

"There's been erosion at the shoreline. The biggest difference, though, is that the forest is gone."

They looked at the green fields dotted with cottages and farmhouses, separated only by small woodlots. It was all beautiful, but tame, certainly not mysterious or dangerous.

"Maybe it happened just because we were here, in the right place at the right time," said Maggie. "Your mother mentioned an old story about the spirit of the people coming back to this spot."

"And we just happened to be the same age as the kids who were lost."

"That old story that we read at Tante Helen's house said the children were never found. Maybe they left a little crack, a little space in history that we could fit into."

"Like two pieces just the right shape and size to fit into a jigsaw puzzle."

After another silence, Maggie asked in a small tight voice, "What happened to them, Marc? What do your history books tell you about that?"

"The Acadians? I think they were taken to France. Yes, that's where they were going when the *Duke William* sank. They didn't like it there, though. It was a foreign country. They weren't French any more, they were Acadians. Some of them came back to North America after a few years."

"Do you think our families, our Acadian families, came back here?"

"I don't know. We could go to the library and look it up. It was an awfully long time ago. I'm not sure we'd be able to find out."

"There are lots of Acadians living here now," said Maggie, remembering the flags they saw on their drive to Tante Helen's. "We know some of them hid in the forest, but maybe some of the others came back."

"I've just noticed something," said Marc. "We're speaking English."

When they arrived at their own shore, they could see Aunt Kate sleeping in her lawn chair with her hat over her face. Marc's father was hoeing his vegetable garden. When they waved and called, he put down his hoe and came to get Marc.

He stopped abruptly at the bottom of the stairs. "Where are your jeans? And the paddles?"

Maggie and Marc looked at each other.

"The storm," Marc began.

"Oh, yes," said his dad, "the storm that didn't materialize. But what on earth happened to you kids?"

"Oh, just a little surprise dunk," said Maggie quickly before Marc could speak. But Marc understood what she was thinking and he quickly added, "Nothing we couldn't handle, Dad. Sorry about the paddles though."

As the father hoisted his son on his back and began climbing up the steps, Maggie heard Marc say, "After I put my legs on, I'll help you in the garden."

His father paused for a moment, one foot on the next step. He turned his head to Marc with a look of surprise, then pleasure. He said something too softly for Maggie to hear, but father and son both smiled.

Maggie ran up the steps and the path toward the cabin. She paused a moment by Aunt Kate's lawn chair. The woman was gently snoring. Her straw hat had fallen from her face and was resting on her shoulder. Her eyes were shut tight against the sunlight, and sweat was shining in the little valleys of her leathery skin.

Aunt Kate was getting old, Maggie realized. Then she had a sudden thought, so powerful that it made her throat constrict. Aunt Kate never talked about her parents or her growing up years. Maybe she had never had anyone to love her. Maybe that was why she often seemed cold and grouchy.

Maggie shut her eyes and remembered her Acadian family. She knew she would never feel lost and lonely again. She would always remember their warmth and love. Maybe she was strong enough now to give some of that affection back to Aunt Kate. Gently, so as not to waken her, Maggie placed the hat back on Aunt Kate's forehead so it shaded her eyes from the sun. Then, before moving on, she let her fingers rest for a moment against the wrinkled cheek.

She paused on the doorstep of the cottage and looked around. It was all so beautiful and peaceful. Across the road a herd of Holsteins, fat and sleek, were grazing on lush summer grass. It was an unlikely place for ugly things to have happened, she thought. But ugly things had happened here, nonetheless.

In the days that followed, Marc's parents often remarked on how he had changed. He seemed full of energy and enthusiasm. Happier, more contented. Sometimes, though, he puzzled them — like the time he asked if a pine tree could be planted where he could see it from his bedroom window.

Aunt Kate often said that their vacation seemed to be doing Maggie a lot of good. The child was becoming quite pleasant to have around. When Maggie heard her say that, she smiled.

Maggie and Marc got together every chance they could to talk about their life in the Acadian village. Perhaps because they wanted so much for it to be true, they agreed that their Acadian families likely had returned to their farms on the bay. They looked at the Holsteins across the road and imagined Isabelle there, just as fat and sleek, with her calf at her side.

Maggie pictured Maman, Papa, the boys and the little girls living in a spacious cabin surrounded by fields of grain growing tall in the sun. She always thought of Maman working at her spinning wheel and singing an old song brought from France by the first Acadians, her sweet voice floating on the air, as strong and comforting as love itself.

• • •

July wore on, and it was almost time to leave Prince Edward Island. Maggie didn't want to go. With the passing of only a few short weeks, her memories were already starting to fade. She couldn't quite picture Antonine's face any more. She couldn't remember the exact sound of Papa's laugh. She was beginning to think that perhaps she and Marc had imagined everything after all. It all seemed so dream-like, so fantastic.

The night before Maggie and Aunt Kate were to leave for Fredericton, Marc and his mother came to say goodbye. Maggie took him aside and told him her fears.

"Don't be silly," he said, but she could tell by the way he refused to look her in the eye that he was also wondering if they really had journeyed into the past. They were both sad and quiet.

The next morning Maggie packed while Aunt Kate tidied up the kitchen. Mrs. McKay would be picking them up soon to drive them to the airport. Marc and his father wouldn't be coming because they were busy planting Marc's pine tree near his bedroom window.

As Maggie set her suitcase on the front step, she heard Marc calling her name. She walked around the cabin. He and his father seemed excited. Mr. McKay was digging as if in a frenzy. Shovelfulls of dirt were flying, and Marc was yelling for Maggie to come. She ran up the path.

"What's going on?" Maggie asked.

Marc was so excited that he was laughing as he spoke. "Look, look!" he said. "We were digging a hole to plant the tree and the shovel hit something. So Dad kept digging around it, to see what it was. Look!"

Maggie peered into the hole. Mr. McKay had stopped digging now, and was on his knees clearing the soil away with his hands. He was unearthing something made of metal. Then Maggie saw why Marc was so excited. She began to laugh and her laughter joined his. The sound was so joyous that Mr. McKay stared at them, bewildered.

They were laughing, for there at their feet, exposed to the sunlight for the first time in more than two hundred years, was a bell. An Acadian church bell!

Another Time Travel Adventure
from Ragweed Press

Beyond the Waterfall
by Elaine Breault Hammond

In her second time travel adventure, Maggie finds herself transported to the Canadian prairie of the early 1890s. Mistaken for another girl, she becomes part of a pioneer family ... attending school, doing chores and helping to look after her new family's horses.

Maggie soon befriends Nicholas, one of the "home children" sent to Canada to escape the poverty and starvation in England. Nicholas is being poorly treated by his Canadian host family; he misses his mother terribly and wants to bring her to Canada. Ingenuity and good luck team up to help Maggie and Nicholas in this endeavour, but will Maggie be as lucky when she tries to return to her own time and place?

ISBN 0-921556-68-3 $7.95